MW00752955

The

FAMILY HITCHCOCK

PUBLIC LIBRARY

SEP 2011

SOUTH BEND, INDIANA

Story by
**MARK LEVIN & JENNIFER
FLACKETT**

Written by **DAN ELISH**

KATHERINE TEGEN BOOKS
An Imprint of HarperCollins Publishers

Katherine Tegen Books is an imprint of HarperCollins Publishers.

The Family Hitchcock

Copyright © 2011 by Mark Levin and Jennifer Flackett

All rights reserved. Printed in the United States of America.
No part of this book may be used or reproduced in any manner
whatsoever without written permission except in the case of brief
quotations embodied in critical articles and reviews. For information
address HarperCollins Children's Books, a division of HarperCollins
Publishers, 10 East 53rd Street, New York, NY 10022.
www.harpercollinschildrens.com

Library of Congress Cataloging-in-Publication Data is available.
ISBN 978-0-06-189394-0 (trade bdg.)

Typography by Amy Ryan
11 12 13 14 15 LP/RRDB 10 9 8 7 6 5 4 3 2 1
❖
First Edition

For Ellen and Lindsay,
who make everything more fun

The
FAMILY HITCHCOCK

CHAPTER ONE

When she was younger, Maddy Hitchcock didn't mind that her little brother was so smart. It was fun in a way—sort of like living with an around-the-clock walking, talking circus freak show.

Step right up and meet Benji Hitchcock, the three-year-old kid who can already do long division!

Meet the four-year-old wonder boy who knows that there are three hundred and fifty-three species of sharks!

Hear the boy genius play Beethoven's first ten piano sonatas by memory!

That was Benji—with the exception of sports, he was good at practically everything. Though she never really said it, Maddy was even proud of him. On Sunday mornings, she liked to hear him read the front page of the *New York Times* to his parents. And who else could construct a four-foot-tall Death Star out of Legos?

To tell the truth, Maddy wasn't sure exactly what had made her feelings go sour. Maybe Benji had always been annoying but she had just never noticed? Maybe it was just part of growing up?

"It's hormones." That's what her best friend, Grace Richards, had said on the first day of seventh grade. "I mean, we're in junior high now. We have algebra homework, French verbs to conjugate, boys who like us, and more than a thousand friends each on Facebook. Who has time for a nine-year-old brother?"

"I love him," Maddy said. "But the boy-genius act is getting old. Last night he sang the clarinet part of Mozart's fortieth symphony at dinner. It's like I've spent my life competing for attention with a champion puppy."

Sure, Maddy's parents tried to give her equal time— she knew that. Her father was always ready with a compliment on a good report card. Her mother had showed at every one of her gymnastics competitions. But it was a losing battle. Creative and bright just didn't hold a candle to cute and brilliant. But did that mean that a teenage girl, smart in her own right, had to put up with it anymore?

"Here's what you do," Grace said. "Lay down a new law."

Maddy chewed on that for a minute. "You really think I can? After all these years?"

Grace pointed to the school entrance. "Look at that sign. HILLSIDE TOWNSHIP JUNIOR HIGH. That's us. Big girls." She shot Maddy a look. "Don't tell me you can't handle a fourth-grade boy?"

So Maddy handled him. It was the following morning at breakfast. Maddy was focused on a bowl of granola and a dog-eared copy of *Our Bodies, Ourselves.* Benji was scrolling websites on his laptop.

"Guess what, Mads," Benji said. "There's this really cool thing online about black holes."

Maddy knew full well what the old her would have done—flashed an affectionate grin and said, "Tell me everything!"

But that model had been retired. No need to be overly harsh. Just the facts, ma'am.

"Look, Benji."

"What?"

Maddy sighed. Her brother really did look like a champion puppy. He was that cute. That eager to please.

"I'm thirteen now," she began. "I have algebra homework, French verbs to conjugate, two boys who like me, and more than a thousand friends on Facebook."

"Yeah?" Benji said. As usual, his thick glasses were slightly forward on his nose. His hair was uncombed. "So?"

Maddy shook her head. How could a child so intellectually gifted be so clueless?

"So this," Maddy said. "No offense, but I just don't have time for black holes right now."

Benji looked confused. "Then when?"

Maddy forced a smile. "I'll get back to you on that, OK?"

She buried her face back in her granola. When her cell phone rang, she sprang to her feet, already talking, and all but speed-walked down the hall to her room.

She hated to do it, but sometimes a girl had to look out for herself.

As for Benji, it didn't take him long to blame it all on junior high, an institution that had magically transformed his once sweet sister into a moody, illogical jerk. After a few failed attempts at conversation, he deduced that the safest course of action was to lay low and pretend she didn't exist—a state of affairs that suited Maddy just fine. And so from fall through winter the Hitchcock siblings shared the same roof, food, and parents but little else. Maddy spent time at home with iChats, fights with her mom, texts, more fights with her mom, fights with her dad, and, when required, homework. Benji spent his time devising a computer program that measured global climate change by ZIP code and perfecting Chopin's *Revolutionary* Etude in C Minor. Sibling communication ran the gamut from "Where's the toothpaste?" to "Give it."

Until the first week of spring break. The last remnants of snow were melting in the Hitchcock front yard. Benji was in his bedroom reading a biography of Sir Isaac Newton when he heard an impatient rap on his door.

"Yeah?"

"Come on, Benj. You know who it is."

The boy's heart nearly stopped. *Maddy!* His first thought was that she was stopping by to rip out his heart with a sharpened barrette. Earlier that morning, while trying to rewire his computer, he had accidentally cut the power to her room. He had fixed the problem in minutes, but who knew what damage had been done? Had his sister been cut off mid-IM to Grace? Had her blow-dryer fritzed out in the middle of a particularly wet strand of hair?

"Yeah?" he stammered.

"Come on, Benji. Open up!"

What else could a little brother do? He opened the door. There was Maddy, wearing a pair of bell-bottom jeans, black boots, and a purple top. Her blond hair hung loosely around her face. Even Benji had noticed the change in her over the past year. Though he vaguely understood that older boys thought his sister was pretty—*hot,* even—it was a subject he didn't like to think about.

"What?"

"Hey, can we talk?"

"Sorry if your computer crashed, Mads. I can fix it. I can fix anything. I'll rewire your room. Put speakers in your shower. Put a forty-inch monitor on your ceiling."

Maddy flopped down on his bed.

"Relax. It's not my computer." She smiled. "I'm being nice here, can't you tell?"

To Benji's surprise, his sister's lips were, in fact, curving upward. For a brief moment, Benji was reminded of the sweet girl that he was certain still resided somewhere inside his sister's body.

"What is it?"

"It's Mom and Dad."

"What about them?"

Maddy gave him a knowing look. Yes, Benji was book smart. But she was *life* smart.

"What happens this time every year? What do we plan for?"

Benji got it. The annual family vacation. Every year since he could remember, his father and mother had taken them on some sort of summer trip. When the kids were little, the vacations had been fun—at least, that's how Maddy and Benji remembered them. Hawaii. The Grand Canyon. When Benji was six, they had spent a week in New York seeing shows.

But over the past few years a once-fine family tradition had gone sour. In Disneyland, their mother had made them wear so much sunscreen both children had come back whiter than when they had left. In Alaska, their father took one too many pictures of a grizzly, goading the giant bear into charging their minivan. The year before had been the worst of all. A camping trip to Yosemite fell apart when their dad's port-a-stove set fire to their tent, forcing a visit from a park ranger and a premature escort out of the park.

"I overheard Dad say he wants to go to Rome this

year," Benji said. "He'll burn down the Colosseum."

"I know," Maddy said. "I've got to stay here this July. Grace and I are going to hang at the town pool. You don't know what it's like being a teenager. Junior high is murder. Nothing but cliques and bad makeup. My social pressures have social pressures."

Benji nodded. Something about his sister's desperation touched him. For a brief instant, the brittle facade was gone and Benji caught a glimpse of the Maddy he had once considered a friend. And with his sister opening up, perhaps there was something he could admit to her.

"There's Camp Keys," he said. "It's this sleepaway music and computer camp in Ohio. Look, I'll show you the site." Before Maddy could object, Benji had it up on his screen, a home page filled with pictures of serious-looking boys and girls playing pianos, practicing cellos, and sitting in front of monitors. "I could probably get a scholarship."

To the boy's surprise, his sister seemed proud of him—like when she used to have him name the presidents in order for her friends back when he was in nursery school.

"Nice," she said. "That'd be perfect for you."

"Yeah, tell me about it."

Brother and sister exchanged a smile—their second in months.

"Hey, check out what I'm reading," Benji said. He held out the biography of Sir Isaac Newton as if his sister's approval would make everything in it worth knowing. "Did you know that Newton built the first reflecting telescope? He also developed a theory of color based on the observation that a prism decomposes white light into the many colors that form the visible spectrum."

Benji's mother had warned him about his tendency to spout facts. But how could he help it when he was just that enthusiastic about all the great stuff he was learning? Still, this time he paid a high price. By the time he was finished, Maddy's welcoming smile had faded.

"I've come up with a plan." Once again, she was all business. "It's pretty darned brilliant, too."

"Yeah?" Benji said. "I'm not surprised. You're the smart one."

If Maddy heard her brother's obvious bit of flattery, she didn't acknowledge it.

"So get ready," she said. "You'll find out at dinner."

"At dinner? Come on, Mads. Give me a hint. What do we do? A hunger strike? A sit-in?"

Benji couldn't remember the last time she had seemed so pleased with herself.

"Just back me up, OK?"

Benji knew his sister well enough to know when further questioning was pointless. "You got it."

Still, for the third time that morning, there was the smile. Had the ice broken? Probably not. But Benji knew that for the next few hours, a truce had been called. He would have to settle for that. No more snippy comments or fear of death at the hands of a sharpened barrette. Sister and brother were a team, brought together for a larger purpose. As their eyes met, there was a quiet confidence that this year would be different. Come July, Maddy would be doing her tan teen thing by the pool and Benji would be pale in front of a PC.

"No more last-minute packing," Maddy said.

Benji nodded. "No more plane delays."

"No mutant mosquitoes."

"No wet sleeping bags."

Maddy tousled Benji's hair. "This is our year."

Benji watched his sister swagger back down the hall and disappear into her room.

Yeah, he thought. *Our year.*

CHAPTER TWO

That afternoon, Maddy ran a series of increasingly detailed searches for online bathing suits, flip-flops, and suntan lotion. Down the hall, Benji took a virtual tour of the Camp Keys grounds, downloaded the application, recorded himself playing Mozart's First Piano Sonata, and typed a draft of his own recommendation letter. But come dinnertime, the Hitchcock children were to learn a lesson on the perils of overconfidence.

On the surface, Roger Hitchcock was a perfectly reasonable man, the sweetest of dads. He didn't throw fits over bad grades or force on rain boots in a drizzle. He looked the other way when an hour of TV turned into two. But just because Maddy and Benji's father let the little things slide didn't make him a pushover. When the chips were down, the usually affable Roger could be as unmovable as the Great Wall of China. And nothing was more important to him than the annual vacation, a time each year when his family could get to know each other a little bit better and just plain have fun.

So what if he had torched their pup tent in Yosemite? Who cared if the ranger at the scene had asked that he never return? By the time the family had returned to their Chicago home the past summer, Roger was already planning the next trip. It would be bigger and better than ever. Which meant one thing: When Maddy and Benji sat down to plates of lasagna that night, they never stood a chance.

"So Dad," Maddy began. "Benji and I have been thinking."

The Hitchcock parents exchanged a surprised glance. After half a year of the silent treatment, their children had been thinking? *Together?*

"About what?" Mrs. Hitchcock asked.

Rebecca Hitchcock was blond like her daughter

and still beautiful at age forty. Married to a man who was almost pathologically easygoing, she had assumed the role of the responsible parent who made sure that homework was finished and vegetables eaten. She could be grumpy about the little things—a decade of unmade beds and scuffed floors had driven her to yoga and Pilates—but Maddy and Benji thought that their mother might be a strong ally in their push to remake their summer plans. On the return trip from Yosemite, she had filled in the empty squares of the in-flight Sudoku with the words *"Never Again! No! No! No! No!"*

Maddy took a deep breath. With so much at stake, she was suddenly more nervous than she had anticipated.

"It's like this, Dad," she said. "Benji and I have been thinking about the economy."

Roger stopped midchew.

"The what?"

"The economy," Maddy repeated.

She looked imploringly at Benji. Though he didn't know where his sister was going, he picked up his cue.

"America's gross national product is down," the boy said with a grave nod.

Roger washed down his food with a glass of water, then smiled. "I'm aware of that."

"People are suffering," Maddy said.

"Losing their jobs," Benji added.

Maddy appreciated how fast her brother was getting with the program.

"The ranks of the unemployed are growing daily," the boy went on.

The children saw their mom shoot their father another glance.

"What's this about?" Rebecca said.

Maddy took another deep breath. Time to go for the kill.

"The market, Dad."

Maddy could tell from the pained look in her father's eyes that she had struck a chord. Roger made his living trading corn futures. A few weeks earlier, a plague of lice had wiped out half of America's crop.

"Oh, sweetie," Rebecca said. "Are you worried that we don't have enough to make ends meet?"

"Things like that happen all the time in my business," Roger said, patting his mouth with a napkin. "It comes with the territory."

"Times are tough, but we'll be OK," Rebecca said.

"Oh, I know we will, Mom," Maddy said.

"Then what's the problem?" Roger asked.

By that point, Benji was wondering the same thing.

As smart as he was, he wasn't exactly sure where Maddy was headed.

"No problem, Dad," Maddy said. Suddenly her heart was beginning to pound. But she was almost home. Better spit out the rest and hope for the best. "It's just that in these difficult times, Benji and I wanted to say that we're willing to sacrifice this year's annual vacation. You know, for the good of the family."

For a moment, Roger's face was unreadable. The two children's eyes met. Had they gone too far? Was the father who never yelled about to pound the table with his fists and rant about the joys of family togetherness? Apparently not. Finally, Roger shook his head with a grateful smile.

"Amazing," he said, looking across the table at his wife. "Not many children would be willing to sacrifice something so important to them for our sake."

Benji exchanged a glance with his sister, then looked at his dad.

"So that means we'll stay home this year?"

Maddy found herself holding her breath. For a brief moment, there was hope.

"Stay home?" Roger cried. "What kind of father would I be if I let a little thing like money get in the way of our special family time? I would never do that.

No, never fear, Hitchcocks!" He raised a finger to the ceiling. "I've already made plans."

The kids exchanged a glance. Each thought the other had never looked so stricken. Rebecca seemed just as surprised—and unhappy.

"Plans, dear?" she asked, voice trembling.

"Why, yes," her husband replied nervously. "I was going to surprise you." He turned quickly to Maddy. "You were right about needing to save money this year, Mads. So guess what, everyone? I arranged a house swap!"

The girl blinked. Didn't they usually stay in a hotel?

"A what?"

Roger wagged his head enthusiastically. "You heard me. For a week in July we'll be living in Paris in the home of Xavier Vadim and his family."

Now Rebecca blinked. "We're going to Paris?"

Maddy couldn't tell if her mother was happy or sad. But she didn't have time to worry about it. She had questions of her own. They all did.

"This Vadim family is going to stay in *our* house?" Maddy asked.

"Right!"

"In our rooms?" Benji asked.

"You got it. Relax. It's all good. He's a chemistry professor."

"Where did you meet him?"

"It was simple, Mads. Vacationswap.com."

"A website?" Maddy said. "This Vadim guy could be a ten-year-old boy, for all you know. Or a serial-rapist-vegetarian-robber-murderer."

"Just as long as they don't rifle through our closets," Rebecca said.

"Ditto my computer," Benji said. "Or use my music for scrap paper or knock over my Lego Death Star."

"Relax," Roger said. "We'll lock away what we don't want them to use. And you don't have to worry that the flight over will break the bank. I booked the tickets using frequent-flier miles."

Rebecca narrowed her eyes. She knew from hard experience what the words "frequent-flier miles" could mean.

"We *are* flying direct, right?"

Maddy could hear the irritation in her voice. She was angry—and rightfully so—for having been kept out of the loop on the family's summer plans. To the children's alarm, their father didn't answer immediately but dug into another piece of lasagna.

"Dad?" Benji said once his father had swallowed. His voice trembled.

Roger washed down his food with a swallow of

water. "Well, there are some minor connections."

"Some?" Maddy asked.

"Three, actually."

"Three!?!"

Maddy and Benji hadn't heard their mother shriek that loudly in months.

"Rebecca, it'll be fine," their father said. "We fly from Chicago to Philly to Miami to London to Paris. Oh, wait." He laughed embarrassedly. "That's four, isn't it?"

Rebecca stood, her face twisted into a horrible grimace. "Four?"

Her children worried she was going to either throw her lasagna at their father's face or dive for his neck across the dining-room table. Instead, she collapsed back in her chair and buried her head in her hands.

"Relax, sweetie," Roger said. "It's going to be fun! Gay Paree! Maddy can practice her French."

"I got a C-minus."

"That's why I said *practice*! Come on, people! This is amazing! Oh, wait a second."

"What?" Maddy said.

"I forgot a minor detail."

"What detail?" Rebecca asked. "What detail?"

Roger swallowed. "After London there's a quick stop in Amsterdam."

"Five connections!?"

Rebecca rose from the table like a ghost, lurched to her left, then teetered to her right before stumbling blindly out of the room, her face twisted in a silent scream. A moment later they heard the door to the master bedroom slam. As Maddy and Benji sank deeper into their chairs, Roger cleaned the last bit of lasagna from his plate.

"Delicious meal," he said. *"Pourquoi pour les dessertes?"*

CHAPTER THREE

Despite his impressive intelligence and musical talent, Benji was still a nine-year-old boy at heart. Sitting on his desk alongside his books on global warming and the history of Western chamber music was a stack of baseball cards, a Slinky, and a container of Silly Putty. On the wall by his bed were posters of the 2011 Cubs and Bulls. On his bed stand stood his famed Lego Death Star. At night he slept in Spider-Man pajamas.

Only not in his own bed. Starting at age three, Benji had gotten in the habit of waking in the middle of the night, stumbling half asleep down the hall to his parents' room, then crawling under the covers at the foot of their bed. In the beginning, Roger had dutifully roused himself and carried his son back to his own room. But when Benji continued to arrive night after night with the regularity of a punctual train, Roger and Rebecca resigned themselves to sharing their bed—a situation that gave young Benji a bird's-eye view of his parents' evolving relationship. If he had been a bit older, he might have found what he saw every morning troubling: Roger and Rebecca Hitchcock never woke in each other's arms—they hadn't done that for years. In fact, they rarely even slept facing each other but passed the nighttime hours back-to-back, each clutching a pillow. Which was exactly how they were sleeping on the morning of July 6—departure day for France—when the alarm went off at seven a.m. sharp.

"OK, Hitchcocks!" Roger called. For someone who had been sound asleep a few seconds earlier, he sounded weirdly awake—then again, he had been looking forward to this day for months. He rubbed the sleep from his eyes and glanced at the clock. "We leave for the airport in exactly ninety-seven minutes!"

The three months since the now infamous "dinner of the five connections" had passed quickly. Though Benji was still sorry about missing out on Camp Keys, with a short pep talk from his dad he had quickly gotten on board with the idea of the Paris house swap.

"How's my wingman?" Roger called, looking down the bed.

Benji rubbed his eyes and reached for his glasses. "Good to go, Dad."

"Nice." Roger nudged his wife's back. "Come on, Rebecca! Time to take this show on the road."

In theory, Rebecca had quickly grown to love the idea of a Paris vacation. But she was so riddled with worries—the cost, how her kids would get along, how she and Maddy would get along, the language barrier—that she found it hard to make the leap to actual ongoing enthusiasm. Now she buried her head under a pillow.

"Gimme five more minutes. The plane doesn't leave until one fifty-five."

"International flight," Roger said. "Long-term parking. We gotta be there two hours early."

With that, he all but bounded out of bed and began to straighten the sheets.

"What in the world are you doing?" Rebecca asked.

"Just making the bed."

Finally, Benji saw his mother's face appear from under the pillow. He had seen the expression before, a mixture of intense irritation and exasperation.

"While I'm in it?"

Roger forced a smile. "Then get up. We're at ninety-six minutes and counting." He scratched his side and looked at Benji. "Wingman, you're in charge of passports."

"You got it, Dad."

"You de man!"

"No, you de man!"

As father and son slapped five, Rebecca rolled to a sitting position and reached for her bathrobe.

"That's progress!" Roger said. "Now listen, everyone. I already left clean hand towels for the Vadims in all the bathrooms, so if you wash your hands, dry them on your pants. OK, now. Time to wake Maddy."

"You start," Rebecca said with a yawn. "Then I'll take over."

Benji knew that waking his sister was often a two-parent job. Where he was a sleepwalker, Maddy was a sleep-later, prone to stay up all hours on Facebook; waking her for school was often a half-hour drag-out fight. He could only imagine how hard it would be to get her upright for the purpose of putting her on a plane headed away from her cherished pool. But Roger was undaunted. Still in his pajamas, he strode purposefully down the hall and rapped sharply on his daughter's door. Benji trailed behind for a front-row seat.

"OK, Mads!" Roger called. "*La vacatione* is about to *commence!* Day of the big house swap, *ma chérie!*"

Thwap!

Roger and Benji exchanged a glance. Had Maddy really thrown a shoe at her door?

"Leave me alone!"

"Maddy!" Roger called. "We're at ninety-five minutes. Your mother will check in on you in exactly thirty seconds."

Maddy lay back on her bed and closed her eyes, despairing. Though she would never admit it, as the end of the school year approached she had secretly looked forward to seeing Paris. Who wouldn't want to check out the Mona Lisa, walk by the Seine, and eat chocolate crepes, even if it was with her parents and little brother?

Then, on the last day of school, everything changed. First came the news that Noah Willis and Alex Mackie, two ninth graders with impressive biceps, had gotten summer jobs as lifeguards. Suddenly every week at the pool seemed doubly precious. Now Grace and the rest of her friends would have a leg up on being the first of their group to date a high-schooler—no mean feat.

But that wasn't all. During the final lunch of the year, word had spread around the cafeteria that Noah was having a blowout party in just a few weeks. Then, to Maddy's absolute delight, shock, and amazement, the older boy had approached her in the parking lot after the last bell.

"Maddy, right?"

Maddy gave Grace's hand a tight squeeze. How was it possible that a mere boy could make her so unspeakably nervous? Even if he did have bluish gray eyes, thick hair, and a cleft?

"Yeah?" she said. "I mean, yes. Maddy. Me."

Noah glanced to his right as though looking to an invisible wingman for moral support. Grace shoved Maddy lightly forward.

"So you know my party next month, right?" Noah went on finally.

"Right."

"Well . . ." He paused.

Maddy looked at Grace, then back at Noah.

"Yeah . . . ?" she said.

"You're coming, right?"

With a raucous "yes!" a split second from exploding joyously into the air, Maddy felt her heart crumble. *Paris!* Who cared about the Mona Lisa, chocolate crepes, or the Eiffel Tower compared to an invite to a party from a ninth grader?

Now she opened her eyes and stared up at the ceiling, remembering the look on Noah's face when she broke the news. He had actually looked bummed—over her! But the look on Grace's face was altogether different. Though her friend did her best to act disappointed on Maddy's behalf, Maddy saw the slight smile and crinkle around her eyes. Was Grace secretly happy that Maddy would be out of the picture so she could horn in on Noah for herself? No doubt.

Suddenly a short week in Paris seemed endless—every second counted.

"Maddy, dear! Come on. We have to get to the airport."

Maddy sat up in bed and sighed. Her *mother*, the real thorn in her side. For every annoying thing her brother did, her mom did three more. Which was doubly painful because they had once been close. But over the past year, mother-daughter communication had gone into freefall. There were days when Maddy felt as though her mind were exploding along with her body—days when she wanted to tell her mother everything. Her emotions swooped high and low like a deranged bird's. But her mother did it every time. Whenever Maddy geared up to bare her soul, Rebecca managed to say or do something irritating.

"I'm telling you, it's the hormones."

That was Grace's answer to everything. But couldn't hormones be controlled? What better time than now to call a truce in the year-long impasse in mother-daughter relations? After all, if Maddy knew anything, it was that she'd need her mom's support if she had any hope of staying home.

"OK," she told herself, sitting up in bed. "Be nice."

"Maddy!"

"Coming, Mom."

She brushed a hand through her hair and swung open the door. Her mother was standing before her in a bathrobe.

"Are you packed?" Rebecca asked. She glanced into the room. "And cleaned?"

Maddy looked behind her. Her room looked like ground zero for a hand-grenade test site. "Getting there. But Mom . . . listen, can we talk?"

"Now?"

"Yeah. Is that OK?"

While her default reaction had been suspicion, Rebecca allowed herself a thin smile. Perhaps the timing wasn't great, but was Maddy ready to confide in her again? Like old times? "What is it, dear? We do have a plane to catch."

Maddy drew in a deep breath. Time to go for broke. "Listen, Mom. I've been thinking. You let me stay here with Grace and I'll make all the beds, mow the lawn, and take out the trash all summer."

Rebecca's thin smile tilted downward.

"I'll throw in French tutoring," Maddy said. "I'll go once a week. No, twice a week until September."

"Not this again, Mads." Rebecca sighed. "Tutoring is no substitute for a trip to Paris. If you want extra help in French, we'll see if we can get you a tutor when we get home. You've got to get that C-minus up."

Usually, a mention of grades made Maddy furious. Now she forced herself to stay calm. Perhaps she needed to change tactics? Rebecca was already turning back to her room to get changed.

"Mom."

Rebecca stopped. "Yes?"

"There's this . . . this boy."

Rebecca blinked. Was her daughter actually offering up personal information? She took a step back up the hall. "What?"

"A boy," Maddy said. "And his name is Noah and

he's having a party." Maddy paused. "He invited me. Personally."

Maddy saw her mother's eyes open wide with a wisp of pleasure. Maddy held her breath and awaited the verdict.

"That's wonderful, dear," her mother said. "Will his parents be home?"

"Come on, Mom. I don't know. But he's in ninth grade. He can handle it."

"Well, when is it?"

"This weekend."

Maddy saw her mother register what Maddy was really asking.

"*This* weekend?"

"Mom! Please!"

Rebecca sighed again. Why did she always get put in the position of being the bad guy? "Noah will still live here when you get home."

"Righto!" her father called, hurrying by with a toiletry kit. "Remember! You're a Hitchcock first!"

Rebecca put a hand on her daughter's shoulder. "Sorry, Maddy. Your father is right. I want to hear more about Noah. But family first."

Her mother tried to pull her close, but Maddy withdrew as if her mother's arms were toxic. "Oh God,

Mom! I open up to you and you give me the family togetherness speech? Excuse me while I puke myself."

She slammed the door. Rebecca tried the handle. It was locked.

"Maddy! Maddy! Open up! Come on, young lady!"

A moment later Roger hurried back up the hall and put his face to the door. "Maddy? Pack a change of clothes in carry-on. You know how you get motion sickness."

That suggestion was greeted by the sound of violent retching. If Roger was concerned, he didn't show it. Instead, he turned to Rebecca and winked.

"She'll be there."

The next hour passed in a mad flurry. Bowing to the inevitable, Maddy emerged from her room. Showers were taken, hair washed, clothes put on. Though they had started two days earlier, there was still plenty to be packed. When it became obvious even to Roger that the first suitcase he had picked wasn't large enough to hold what the family needed, everything was dumped out onto the floor, then repacked into one that was bigger. Books, sunglasses, iPods, and snacks were crammed into carry-ons. At the same time, last-minute preparations were made to get the house ready for their guests.

While Roger had already carefully cleared out two of his drawers for Xavier Vadim's use, Rebecca frantically moved half of her shirts, slacks, and dresses out of her closet to make room for Beatrix Vadim's clothes. In their own rooms, Maddy shoved the mess on her floor under her bed and Benji cleared out his shelf of baseball cards.

And then there were the untouchables—the things each Hitchcock didn't want the Vadims to see or use. Benji put a password protocol on his computer and locked his music inside the piano bench. Rebecca hid her favorite shoes. Maddy shoved her diary into the air-conditioning vent. Roger tucked away his best wine.

Which left the family pictures. With exactly twenty-two minutes until departure, Roger came upon Rebecca hustling through the house with an armload of family portraits lifted from the walls.

"What in the world?" Roger asked. "The pictures, too?"

"So maybe it's overkill, " Rebecca said defensively, "but I don't want strangers we met on the internet who might be serial-rapist-vegetarian-robber-murderers look-ing at all of our photos."

Roger sighed. Over the past three months, he had tried to be patient. In truth, he understood his wife's concerns. It *was* a bit strange to be opening their home to complete strangers, even ones who seemed as refined and trustworthy as the Vadims. But was it really necessary to leave the walls completely barren? Where was the trust? Just as Roger was about to say something, the picture at the top of the pile caught his eye—a snapshot of happy days, when Maddy was nine and Benji five—the greatest Hitchcock vacation of them all: Maui.

"Wow," he said. "Remember this? Back when I could lift Maddy on my shoulders and we could afford hotels?" He smiled, remembering. "Look at Maddy doing gymnastics on the beach."

Rebecca allowed herself a small smile. True, both kids had gotten sunburned and the coffee at the hotel was weak, but all in all, it was one of the good ones. But the happy memories were soon clouded by ongoing anxieties.

"Gymnastics," she said with a rueful smile. "Which she quit after one year."

"No, no," Roger said. "She took gymnastics for three years. She could do some awesome flips."

Rebecca smiled. "She was invited to a party by a boy, you know."

"She told you that?" Roger asked.

Rebecca nodded. "Maybe she's ready to open back up to me?"

Before Roger could respond, a voice pierced the hallway: Maddy's.

"Just so we're clear, family members! I'll go on this stupid vacation because I have no choice! But let it be known that I am being dragged against my will by parents who wouldn't know the right thing to say if it did a tap dance on their head, then bit them on the butt!"

Door slam.

Roger forced a smile. "She'll get over it. You'll see."

Rebecca frowned. "All I want is for this vacation to be halfway decent. Is that too much to ask?"

"No," Roger said. "And it will be. You'll see."

He gave his wife a quick kiss, then turned down the hall.

"Sorry to hear you're unhappy, Maddy, but it's time to move! On the road in twenty minutes!"

The chips were down. On the homestretch, the family went into overdrive.

Remembering they hadn't eaten breakfast, Roger threw four frozen bagels into the toaster oven and set it to high. Outside, Benji lugged the trash into the garage for pickup and fell backward into the garden when the neighbor's Corgi yapped loudly against the chain-link fence that separated the two homes. Terrified, he crawled back to the house and slammed shut the door.

"God," Maddy said. "You make Napoleon Dynamite look like a stud."

"Lay off," Benji said, gasping for breath. "I've got cynophobia. Fear of dogs. It's a diagnosed condition."

"Your conditions have conditions," Maddy said, and whipped off a furious text to Grace: *Tried to talk to Mom. She totally doesn't get me.*

In the master bedroom, Rebecca made a last-minute decision to pack a pair of sneakers.

"Ready then?" Roger said, running in from the kitchen. "Let's load this sucker and hit the road."

Easier said than done. Full to the brim, the larger suitcase wouldn't close. In seconds Roger had the two kids in the room. With some quick negotiating, each family member agreed to take out one article of clothing. Even then, Benji had to sit on the suitcase before Roger could manage to snap it shut.

"Yes!" he shouted. "Done!" He stood tall, grinning wildly. "OK, Hitchcocks! Five minutes and counting! Who wants to help me roll this bad boy into the car?"

The answer was obvious—Benji wanted to help. But the boy never had a chance to open his mouth. An ear-splitting wail of a siren filled the house. The four Hitchcocks stood still, stunned. Maddy whispered what everyone was thinking.

"The smoke alarm."

Rebecca's face clouded over. "Not another port-a-stove?"

Roger's eyes went wide. "No, the toaster oven! The bagels!"

He barreled out of the room, Benji hot on his heels. In the kitchen, a small but smoky fire was burning in the center of the toaster oven.

"Tell me this isn't happening!" Roger cried. "Not on the day of the house swap!"

In a flash, he unplugged the oven from the wall.

"Here!" Benji said, and tossed him two oven mitts.

In seconds, Roger had them on his hands, picked up the still smoking oven, and ran frantically for the backyard. There, father and son stomped on it until the fire was out, leaving it a charred, smoking heap.

Roger wiped his brow and patted Benji on the back. "That was close."

"Yeah, Dad. Wow."

Roger smiled. "Nice work, wingman."

Benji nodded. "Thanks, Dad."

"Uh, Roger? Benji?"

Father and son turned toward the house. Rebecca and Maddy were by the door to the backyard. Standing behind them, in a well-tailored gray suit, was a handsome man with salt-and-pepper hair. Walking out the door was an elegant woman with impeccable makeup in a stunning blue dress. Gripping her leg was a boy, about six years old, in a plaid shirt, shorts, and sandals.

"My apologies if we are early," the man said in a thick French accent. "But our plane caught strong headwinds."

"Isn't this simply wonderful, dear?" Rebecca said, forcing a smile. "The Vadims are early!"

CHAPTER FOUR

Exactly three hours and twenty-two minutes later, a Boeing 737 took off from Chicago's O'Hare Airport. Crammed together, side by side in the second-to-last row, sat the family Hitchcock.

"We're golden," Roger said, glancing at his watch. "We should make our next flight with an hour and twelve minutes to spare."

But no amount of advance planning could ward off bad weather. Though Chicago skies were clear, thunderstorms around the Philadelphia airport delayed their landing, which meant the family barely had time to stop for a cheesesteak before sprinting for their connecting flight to Miami.

"Made it!" Roger called, flopping into his seat, again in the second-to-last row. "Every trip needs a little drama, right? Worry not! From now on, it's all us!"

Once again, the father who had worked so hard to ensure that the vacation went off without a hitch had spoken too soon. Though the weather had cleared, mechanical problems with the plane's air-conditioning system kept the flight in the gate for three hours. Rebecca wasn't pleased. By the time the family landed in Miami, she was a woman on a mission. "One more flight," she muttered, stalking out of the plane toward the ticket agents. *"One. More. Flight!"* With a flurry of well-timed tears and a few choice words, Rebecca booked her family on a direct flight to Paris—no extra charge.

"Nice, honey!" Roger said. Truthfully, after fifteen years of marriage, he still found occasional exposures to his wife's "take no prisoners zone" slightly terrifying. He laughed nervously. "Next time I'll let you make the arrangements."

By that point, there was no one in the family—not even Benji—who felt confident that there would ever be a "next time." Exhausted and stressed, the family was barely on speaking terms. As the Paris-bound 757 took off from the Miami airport, Rebecca leaned back in her chair, snapped a black mask over her eyes, and curled up in one of the airline blankets. Roger sighed. Even on the plane, she instinctively turned her back on him. Needing to feel the glow of some sort of family affection, he glanced over his shoulder to the seats directly behind them. Benji was deep into a book on Einstein, and Maddy was rereading her text in-box.

"Hey, Mads," he said.

As expected, she didn't look up or reply. Undeterred, Roger simply soldiered on.

"So we're off, huh?" Roger said. Like his wife, he never knew quite what to say to his daughter. Not anymore. It was painful, considering that she had once been a certified daddy's girl, the parent she ran for with a scraped knee or a nightmare. "Reading anything interesting?"

Maddy's eyes remained glued to the screen.

"How my parents are ruining my life."

Swallowing hard, Roger made a quick decision to backtrack from his daughter and focus on his son. Benji was always good for an encouraging word.

"Hey, wingman. How's it going?"

Benji frowned. "Not too good."

Roger blinked. Perhaps this was even worse than he had feared. Had the troublesome early phase of the trip dampened his enthusiasm for all things Parisian?

"What's wrong, sport?"

As it turned out, something more consequential than a family vacation was on his son's mind. With a worried frown, Benji tapped his book. "Einstein just discovered the theory behind nuclear fusion."

"So?"

Benji's eyes went wide. "So? Dad, nuclear fusion paved the way for nuclear weapons."

Roger nodded. There had to be some sort of good spin to put on that.

"True, buddy. But think of all the good things Einstein invented, too. Like the lightbulb."

"That was Edison."

Roger forced a smile. Wrong—again.

"Of course." With nothing else to say, he went for the old standby. "Try to get some rest, OK, buddy?"

Benji nodded but kept reading. Roger faced back forward. For a moment he considered trying to chat with his wife. But he could see by the gentle rise and fall of her blanket that she was already asleep. With nothing else to do, Roger leaned back in his chair and tried to get comfortable. Might as well get some shut-eye himself, he thought. Everything would be better with a little rest.

Not surprisingly, Maddy didn't share her father's optimism. As his seat angled sharply toward her lap, she finally looked up from her cell and grimaced. So far, the trip had been even worse than she had anticipated: a knock-down, drag-out horror show. And not just the flights and the delays. The actual travel had been cake compared to the true nightmare that had occurred at their home after the Vadims' arrival. Maddy winced. She should have known how it would go. How mortifying it would be to watch her father fall all over himself, vainly trying to impress people twenty times more cultured. Even worse, trying to speak in French!

"Meeting you is *fantastique!*" he had said while giving them a quick tour of the house. "Now let's *observez ma sal de bain!*"

To their credit, they had tried. But the Vadims simply hadn't been able to suppress a smile.

"What'd I say?" her father asked.

Even the C-minus student knew.

"You asked them to observe your bathroom," Maddy said grimly.

Then things got worse. Not only were the Vadims unfailingly polite, sophisticated, and well groomed—

they were also disgustingly in love.

"Here's *la chambre principale*," Roger said.

In her parents' master bedroom, Beatrix Vadim's eyes lit up. Then, to everyone's surprise, Xavier Vadim kissed her square on the mouth—the kind of kiss she had imagined herself doing in the shallow end of the town pool with Noah Willis.

And there was even more to come. Moments before the Hitchcocks were to leave, Maddy rounded the corner to her bedroom and stopped dead in her tracks. Standing before her was a girl who could have walked off the movie set of *The Addams Family*. Her clothes were black leather. Her skin was pale. Her dark hair was streaked red. Henna tattoos ranged up and down her arms. Maddy saw that one of them was a picture of a skull. Underneath were the words "*Mon Papa*."

"Ah!" Monsieur Vadim called down the hall. "I see you've met Veronique!"

Though Maddy prided herself on having cultivated a harsh edge, a single glance made it clear that Veronique had taken teen angst to a place that was truly frightening.

"Maddy," her father said. "Say hello!"

"Uh, *bonjour*," Maddy said.

Veronique scowled. Clearly, she was just as unhappy to be relocated to Chicago as Maddy was to go to France.

"Veronique!" her mother called down the hall. "Be nice!"

To that, Veronique reached into the inside pocket of her leather jacket. For a moment, Maddy thought her new roommate was about to hand her a present. Instead, the girl pulled out a tube of black lipstick, relined her lips, and walked into Maddy's room. "Ah!" she cried with a thick accent. "*Quel* dump!"

Now, as Benji read beside her and her parents fell into a deep sleep, Maddy reread a string of recent text messages to Grace.

U think Noah likes me?

N's smile is like the sweetest cotton candy.

Then the text she had written a month earlier, a message that still made her wish she was the size of a tree toad.

Noah IMed Janice in English!!! Does he like her? I am too ugly to live.

Maddy cringed. How utterly desperate. And how wrong she had been. Who would have thought that Noah liked *her*? She stared wistfully out the window. Pre-boy life was so much easier. It didn't matter what she wore, what she said, or what music she liked. Now she had to reinvent herself every minute. With a mortified sigh, she scrolled through another group of old texts. Then she started to laugh. At least her boy-obsessed self led to some funny exchanges.

> Grace: I saw Noah thru locker rm. door – no shirt. ☺
> Maddy: Awesome. Did he have MADDY tattooed on his tricep?
> Grace: No, his chest.
> Maddy: I have to see that.

In truth, Maddy had imagined much more than seeing Noah Willis shirtless. There was their first kiss, slow and warm; their election as school fair king and queen; their wedding in center field at Wrigley Field, officiated by Bono. Maddy smiled. Embarrassing, perhaps, but sometimes mere texts weren't even enough to express the full range of her feelings. Occasionally, she liked to put pen to paper, ruminating on Noah's various virtues. Her latest was a poem, "Ode to a Noah," that concluded with these heartfelt lines:

> *Beauty is Noah.*
> *Noah, beauty.*
> *That is all we know on earth,*
> *And all we need to know.*

Suddenly, Maddy felt inspired to put more of her deepest thoughts on paper. But before she could add to her growing opus on the most popular boy in junior high, the busy day took its toll. Despite her best efforts to stay awake, Maddy found herself drifting off—with her cell phone open on her lap.

She awoke what seemed like moments later, her face pressed hard into the side of the seat. Now that the plane was well on its way overseas, the overhead lights were off. Flying through smooth skies, the plane felt completely still, as though it were hanging suspended in space rather than moving forward. For a moment, Maddy didn't know where she was. Once she got her bearings, she shook herself and tried to get comfortable back in her seat. She had been having a wonderful dream. She didn't remember it in total, just a few choice details. The shimmer of pool water. A brilliant smile. A tricep. If she fell back to sleep quickly enough, maybe she could recapture the magic.

But just as she was closing her eyes, she noticed something. Actually, she noticed something's absence—the weight of a phone in her hand. She sat up with a start and looked to the floor, then instinctively glanced to her right. Just as she thought. Sometime after she had dozed off, Benji had decided that the personal life of Maddy Hitchcock held even greater interest than that of Albert Einstein.

"What are you doing?"

Benji's response was everything Maddy might have hoped for. The loud gasp came first. Then he burst out of his chair—or tried to. Held down by the seatbelt, he flopped back against his seat, his glasses now up on his forehead.

"Is your life so dull you need to live through mine? Gimme that!"

She grabbed the phone and looked to see what message Benji had been reading. To her relief, it wasn't one about Noah. Still, it wasn't a text meant for Benji's innocent eyes:

OMG my parents R so getting a divorce.

"Mom and Dad?" he stammered. "Getting a divorce?"

"Benji! That wasn't for you to read."

Benji had more pressing worries than the dubious moral footing of reading someone's texts without permission.

"It can't be," he said. "How do you know this?"

"I just know, all right?" she said. "I don't live in a bubble like you. You still wake up every morning at the foot of Mom and Dad's bed. I live in the United States of real."

Even as she chewed him out, Maddy almost felt bad for him. Benji looked truly shaken, as though his world had just crumbled in his face. His glasses were completely askew. But she was too mad to go soft. Unauthorized text-reading could not be tolerated.

"Just tell me," the boy squeaked. "Is it that they don't do their Saturday night date night anymore?"

"That's one of them."

"What else?"

Maddy sighed. "They don't kiss. At least, I don't see them. Have you?"

Benji thought about it, straining to remember some sort of recent lip-on-lip parental contact. Nothing. He shook his head.

"No," he said.

"Yeah." Maddy sighed again. "Me neither."

Brother and sister were quiet for a moment.

"They used to all the time," Maddy said.

"I know," Benji said. "Remember how Dad used to pick Mom up and twirl her around his head fireman-style and how she would laugh?" Benji shook his head. "Dad would never move out, would he?"

"Well, *he* wouldn't," Maddy said. "It's Mom I'm worried about."

"Why?"

"Well . . ."

"What? Come on! You saw something. I can tell. What was it?"

"Listen, Benji," Maddy said. "Just forget I said anything, OK? I'm probably wrong."

"But you . . ."

"Forget it, OK?"

Maddy buried her face back in her phone. Benji knew better than to keep at her now. His best hope was to wait until they landed, then pester her all through Paris until she broke down and told him what he wanted to know. Of course, that didn't help him now. Especially since Maddy's words had rung true. For instance, why did his parents sleep on opposite sides of the bed? And when was the last time his father had done the fireman lift to his mom? He couldn't remember.

As Maddy scrolled down her list of texts, Benji looked through the seats to his parents. They were both asleep, and his mother's head was resting on his father's shoulder. Benji knew it didn't really mean anything—sound asleep, his mother would have been happy to put her head on any reasonably soft place—but it still gave him hope. Yes, his father could be like a camp director on caffeine and his mother treated life as something to worry about rather than enjoy. But maybe this trip could bring them back together.

Benji picked up his book. If Einstein could figure out how to split the atom, anything was possible.

CHAPTER FIVE

No doubt about it. Benji took after his dad. The boy could find the good in everything. That's all Maddy could think as she clung to the backseat of a careening cab, sandwiched between her father and brother. The moment after landing, the rain had started. Now, through the downpour, Benji was jabbing a thumb at the rain-streaked windows, madly pointing out the Parisian sights like a tour guide gone native.

"Look, Dad! Look! I mean, *Regardez, Papa*! L'Arche de la Défense! Paris is freaking awesome, isn't it!"

Maddy had to admit it: The city was beautiful, even in the rain. She had never seen a wide, open street like the Champs-Elysées or a monument quite as striking as the Arc de Triomphe. But even as she took in the sights, Maddy couldn't help thinking about her friends back home, those girls and boys whose parents didn't break the bank to give their children some sort of summer cultural experience. Grace's father didn't care what she did over the summer, just as long as she stayed out of his hair. Deep down, Maddy didn't want a father that uninvolved. She was lucky to have parents who took her to Europe. But it was hard to focus on the sights with visions spinning through her jet-lagged mind of Grace moving in on Noah. To make the scenery even harder to appreciate, the cabdriver was really moving—which was making her insides move, too. Of all the bad things Maddy had inherited from her mother, car sickness was her least favorite.

"How do you say *slow down?*" Maddy asked.

"You're the French student," her mother chimed from the front seat.

For once, Maddy wished that she was a good one.

"*Vite! Vite!*" she told the driver.

"*Oui, Madmoiselle.*"

He stepped hard on the gas.

"You just said go faster," Benji said.

"Omigod!" Maddy said. "I am so car sick right now."

"Open your window, sweets," Roger said.

"But it's pouring."

The taxi driver swerved, narrowly missing a man running across the street using a copy of *Le Monde* for an umbrella. Maddy groaned.

"*Idiot!*" the driver called.

"Oh my lord! Madeleine Hitchcock! You haven't been strapped in all this time!"

Maddy couldn't believe her ears. Whizzing down one of the most famous and beautiful streets in the world with a physically ill daughter and all her mother could think about was auto safety? Thankfully, her father came to her rescue.

"Becs," he said. There was an unaccustomed edge to his voice. "Give it a little rest."

"A little rest?" Rebecca said.

"Yes," Roger said. "Let's stay cool, OK?"

"Turn around, Mom," Benji said. "You'll get sick, too."

Instead, Rebecca eyed Roger up and down. "Are you OK?"

Maddy and Benji exchanged a quick glance. For a split second, she was worried that her brother was going to blurt out something like, "Of course Dad isn't OK! How could he be when you're about to dump him like a bag of month-old manure? At least, that's what Maddy says." But if Benji was planning on mentioning anything about their conversation on the plane, he was cut off by Roger, who retreated to his default response in the face of anything emotionally unpleasant—a jocular, if forced, enthusiasm, topped off with a "happy voice."

"Oh, no, no," Roger said with a grin. "I'm fine, Becs. Just watching the big bad meter. This ride's turning into a budget buster!"

With that, he leaned forward to speak to the driver.

"*Excusez-moi? Est que . . .* " Giving up quickly, he turned back to Maddy. "You ask him. You're the French speaker."

"I'm also the girl who just told the driver to speed up. I'm the C-minus student, remember?"

"Because you don't apply yourself."

"Because I'm not into it."

"What are you into then?"

"That's easy," Benji said. "Noah Willis!"

"Shut! Up!"

Maddy reached across her father and socked Benji hard in the shoulder.

"Ow!"

"Come on, guys!" Roger said. "Can't we all just get along?"

"God, I am so sick," Maddy said.

"Don't throw up," Benji said. "Because you know what happens when other people throw up. I throw up, too."

"All right, people," Roger said, laughing nervously. "No one is getting sick in this car! *Ne gettez sickez pas.*"

As was becoming more and more the case lately, Roger was unable to control events. Maddy thought that she would be first. But no sooner had Roger finished speaking than Rebecca craned her neck. With a mighty retching sound she vomited all over the dashboard. The cab swerved wildly, this time narrowly missing an old lady carrying a loaf of bread before the cabbie righted the car on the road.

"Mon Dieu!" he cried.

"Pull over!" Maddy called. "Pull over!"

Somehow, the cabbie understood perfectly. With a loud screech, the taxi stopped at La Place de la Concorde, perhaps the most historic square in Paris. Before them stood the Obelisk of Luxor, a seventy-five-foot-tall monolith given to France by the king of Eygpt. But Maddy wasn't well enough to focus on its beauty.

Instead, she kicked open the cab door and vomited violently on the curb. Benji and Roger spilled out after her, barely able to control their own stomachs.

"God," Maddy heard her father say. "Was the plane food really that bad?"

A moment later the very unhappy-looking taxi driver had their bags on the street. Roger took out his wallet and paid the fare. With a shake of his head, the cabbie pointed to the stained front seat and pulled out another few bills—large ones—then sped away in an angry burst of exhaust. Only after the car had left was Maddy able to stumble to a nearby bench.

"You OK, Mads?" Roger said. "Are you well enough to find the Vadims' home?"

"Once I finish saying hello to my guts."

"Where are we going anyway?" Rebecca said. "All I see is miles of traffic."

Maddy frowned. For a brief moment she felt almost sorry for her father. It was as if her mother was enjoying the fact that the trip over had been a disaster, almost as though she had even enjoyed that she had thrown up so she could say "I told you so" later on. Still, this was a case when Maddy had to admit that her mother had a point. The cab had let them off in the middle of one of Paris's busiest streets, with eight lanes of traffic whizzing by and no crosswalks in sight. Once again, Benji the super brother came to the rescue. Reaching into his backpack, the boy took out a giant piece of computer paper and held it up.

"What's that?" Maddy asked.

"A printout of the area from Google Earth," Benji replied. His finger traced over the page and stopped near the center. "We are here. And the Vadims' place, 39 Rue de Solférino, is . . . here! Just a quick lope over the Pont Solférino. That's a bridge across the Seine River. Come on!"

Roger practically exploded with joy.

"Nice, wingman! Onward, Hitchcocks! Time to check out our new digs!"

Maddy struggled to her feet and followed her family up the street to the bridge. The light rain felt good on her face. Now that she was out of the car and had thrown up, she felt better. And even though she had fought with all of her might to stay home, she had to admit that the Seine was a beautiful river. Even romantic. Perhaps she should text a picture or two to Noah to make sure he didn't forget her?

Roger also loved the river. Even though he had pushed for the trip, he was struck by just how much he loved Paris—how beautiful it was, how sophisticated.

Before them stood the Louvre Museum, home of the Mona Lisa, one of the greatest paintings in the world. It was all so wonderful. It made him feel smarter just to be walking down Paris's elegant streets.

Unfortunately, his family didn't seem to share his feelings—at least not yet. Walking across the Seine, Benji called out, *"Allons-y! Allons-y!"* which even Roger knew meant "Hurry!" But Maddy wasn't rushing for anyone. She was snapping a photo with her cell phone.

"Come on, sweetie," Rebecca said. "There will be plenty of time for pictures later."

Maddy didn't answer. Taking her own sweet time, she took a final shot and sent it off.

"Who are you texting, dear?" Roger asked.

"I know!" Benji said.

"Shut up."

The conversation went on from there, but by that point Roger was determined to block out the gripes of his family and focus on the glorious sounds of Paris in the morning. It had finally stopped raining, and the honks of taxicabs, the calls of the food vendors selling fresh baguettes, and the bright shouts of school kids filled the air. And then there were the smells.

"Ah," he said. They had just entered the Seventh Arrondisement, one of Paris's fanciest districts. "Smell that air. I haven't smelled something quite like this since I came here on a Eurorail Pass twenty-two years ago."

Maddy took a deep whiff. "You ask me, it smells like . . . I don't know, sort of like urine."

Roger bit his lip, willing himself to stay calm. "No, that's not urine, Mads," he said, pasting on his best grin. "That is the great metropolis stirring awake, washed by the dewy mist of morning."

To that, Benji tugged on Roger's shirt. "No, Dad," he said. "It *is* urine."

Roger glanced over his shoulder. A homeless man was relieving himself against the side of a building. Rebecca smiled.

"Ah, Europe!" she said. "How glorious!"

Roger frowned but cheered up a moment later when Benji pointed to the side of the next building down.

"Hey, everyone. This is it."

Indeed it was. Roger sighed. Another reprieve! Maddy had to admit, as she peeked through the door, that it looked nice. The facade was constructed out of bright red brick and marble. The lobby was large and well lit. Expensive-looking art hung from the walls. Roger pressed the security code the Vadims had given him into a pad on the side of the wrought-iron front door. The lock clicked.

"Come on, Hitchcocks!" Roger called, pushing the door open. "Our new home is a short elevator ride away."

Once again, Roger found that he had spoken entirely too soon.

"Uh, maybe not, Dad," Benji said.

"What?" Roger laughed. "The Vadims are on the sixth floor, buddy. I don't know about you, but I'm not walking."

"So sorry, *monsieur*," came a voice. "But I am afraid that you are."

Roger looked up. Standing in the elevator was a man in a greasy gray work suit, holding a wrench. His dark scowl perfectly complemented his pierced right eyebrow. "Zes elevator is down for maintenance."

Roger's heart dropped. Even he was beginning to feel some chinks in his pathologically upbeat armor.

"Please tell me you're joking?"

The Elevator Man didn't smile or apologize. "Should be done in a couple of weeks."

Roger closed his eyes and waited for it. Then it came, in tandem.

"A couple of weeks!" Rebecca and Maddy said.

By the time Roger roped them into taking the lead up the circular, narrow flight of stairs, he was all but praying that the apartment would be a veritable shrine. He turned to his son. "You got my back, wingman?"

Benji nodded. "I'm on it."

But half a dozen steps up the stairs, the boy stopped. As a young scientist and musician, he lived in a world of facts, trusting data over feelings. But sometimes even a fleeting impression was too strong to be ignored. Benji sensed that he was being watched. On the first landing, he turned. Standing at the bottom of the stairs was the Elevator Man, staring up, again unsmiling.

"Yes?" Benji said. "What?"

"*Rien, Rien,*" the Elevator Man said. He had a nice enough face, Benji thought, if he would only smile and lose the safety pin through his eyebrow. "Just watching. Making sure you get up OK."

Heart pounding, Benji turned and trotted up the stairs. Another flight up, he glanced back down to the lobby. By that time the man was back in the broken elevator, taking a screwdriver to the control panel. As if on cue, he looked up and met Benji's eyes again. Even from a distance, the pin in his eyebrow looked enormous, as though the cut had been made with a machete. The boy gasped, then turned quickly away, suddenly imagining that the man was a spy, paid by the French government to keep an eye on them. Or maybe he was a member of some weird Parisian cult that kidnapped and tortured unsuspecting tourists.

Benji shook his head. "Stop it," he told himself. "You're being a paranoid freak."

No doubt about it: He was letting his imagination run away with him. The Elevator Man wasn't a spy. He would probably turn out to be a nice guy to have around the building. Someone to recommend fun things to do around the city, or good, cheap restaurants. In fact, hadn't Benji just been rude? Maybe the man *had* been watching to make sure he got upstairs in one piece. Shouldn't he say thanks? Benji leaned over the railing to call *"Merci."* But then he heard it. A scream, loud and piercing, that echoed down the stairwell from the sixth floor.

His mother.

She screamed again.

The Elevator Man could wait.

CHAPTER SIX

Benji took the stairs two at a time, his mind working overtime. He was right about the Elevator Man! Maybe he wasn't a spy but a robber, the lookout man, and his accomplices were upstairs! On a rampage!

Benji heard a third scream.

His sister!

"Hold on!" Benji called. "I'm coming!"

Though the boy hadn't been in a single fight in his entire life, he was determined to defend his family. Who knew where his father was. Maybe already knocked out, or hanging upside down out the window. And his mother and sister? Already tied up in a closet.

I'll take them out with quick, sharp blows to the neck, the boy thought. *Then I'll tie them up with bedsheets, gag them with a croissant, and drag them down the stairs and find a policeman.*

Taking the last flight three steps at a time, he flew across the landing and burst into the apartment, fists clenched, ready to do battle.

But with who? Benji was so surprised it took him a minute to adjust to the scene before him. To his relief, his mother and sister were standing just inside a lavish living room. They seemed to be fine. In fact, he hadn't seen them look so happy in months. His father, too. Roger was leaning against a grand piano, positively glowing.

His mother all but skipped across the room and kissed him on the cheek.

"Oh, Benji! Look! They even have a piano! Isn't it wonderful?"

Again, it took the boy a moment to realize that "it" referred to the apartment. Now that he knew his family was safe, Benji took a look around. Like most nine-year-old boys, Benji had little concern for interior design. But even he could tell the apartment was plush.

The grand salon was enormous. A chandelier hung down from the high ceiling. The furniture was covered with delicately embroidered fabrics.

"Looks even better than on the internet," he said.

"It sure does!" Rebecca said.

Benji was pleased to see his mother's change of mood—but also a bit mystified. It was astonishing what a nice piece of drapery or carpeting could do for a mom's spirits.

"Round one for the Hitchcocks!" Roger crowed. "Their place is nicer than ours."

Rebecca giggled. "I almost feel bad for them."

"I still can't believe that we actually get to live here," Maddy said, poking her head into a giant kitchen, complete with the newest appliances.

"Six glorious nights," Roger said. Then he noticed something. Next to the kitchen was an oak cabinet, locked tight with a silver padlock. "And check it out! They've locked up their personals, too."

"Wow," Benji said. "Interesting."

He was already walking to the piano. He had a decent upright at home, but this looked incredible. A Steinway grand! Without waiting another moment, Benji sat at the bench and launched into the third movement of Beethoven's *Pathétique* Sonata.

"Sounds great, kiddo," his father called from the kitchen.

"You're like George Gershwin," Maddy called, also from the kitchen. "An American in Paris."

"Thanks."

"Boy," Rebecca said. "Xavier Vadim does pretty well for a chemistry professor."

"Maybe there's family money?" Roger said.

"Check it out, Mom!" Maddy said.

"What?"

"Mrs. Vadim has every kind of spice under the sun. She must be some chef."

Rebecca looked. Indeed, the spice rack was lavish, made of dark wood and stoked to the nines. She nudged her daughter on the shoulder.

"Maybe we can cook something while we're here? Like we used to."

Maddy knew her mother was making an effort. Where was the harm in giving a little in return?

"Sure, Mom. We'll cook."

Then she glanced down the hall.

"Go," Rebecca said. "Find your room."

Leaving her mother reveling in the glory of the Vadim kitchen, Maddy wandered toward the back of the apartment. But what would a room belonging to a girl like Veronique Vadim be like? Would there be a giant skull on the door? A "make your own" tattoo machine by her bed? Maybe even a dead body hanging from the ceiling? Suddenly nervous, Maddy walked down a back hallway and peeked in the first door. A broom closet. The next room down was a very ordinary bathroom. But then she came to a blue door with the name "Veronique" written on a plaque in squiggly purple script. Underneath was a picture of a rainbow. Maddy hesitated. A *rainbow*? That didn't seem at all in character with the girl with henna tattoos she had met. Then again, how many other Veroniques could there be in one family?

There'll probably be a shrunken head hanging from the ceiling, Maddy told herself.

Steeling herself for the worst, she pushed open the door. To her surprise, no blood was dripping from the walls. There wasn't a single EMO or Goth poster. Instead, the place was . . . *girly*. The walls were bright pink. There was a canopied bed. By a carefully stacked bookshelf was a poster for a local production of *The Sound of Music*. By the window was a desk where pens and pencils were arranged by color in a jar. A blue rug looked recently vacuumed.

Astonished, Maddy stepped carefully across the rug

and put her suitcase down on the floor by the bed. Was this really Veronique Vadim's room? Maybe the black clothes and bad attitude was an act she was trying on for America. Maddy wandered to the window and glanced at the desk. Next to the carefully arranged pencils was a set of yellow notepads. Now it was official. Embossed on the top right corner of each pad were the words *Du bureau de Veronique.* "From Veronique's desk." Maddy took another long look around the room. Even with the hard and fast proof, it was difficult to connect the way the room was decorated to the girl she had met back in Chicago. It was so strange, Maddy needed to show the rest of her family. But turning for the door, something out the window caught her eye.

In an apartment across a courtyard, a teenage boy was standing at an easel, paintbrush in hand. Maddy pressed her face to the glass and watched him pause for a moment, apply his brush to the canvas, then take a step back to admire his painting, a portrait of a pretty girl with bright red hair. The boy was nice looking, too—tall with a sensitive, serious face. Maddy smiled. It all seemed wonderfully Parisian. Yes, she had fought to stay home, but wouldn't it be nice to live in a country where teenage boys drew romantic pictures of girls they liked? Wouldn't Noah Willis look dashing in a beret, standing in front of the Louvre, painting her for posterity?

Then again, why couldn't a teenage girl get into the creative spirit? She had always felt her poem, "Ode to a Noah," needed another verse. Inspired by the boy across the way, Maddy sat at the desk. She knew what her mother would say if she found her rifling through Veronique's drawers. But wasn't this her room for the next week? Besides, there were times when inspiration could not be denied. She needed paper and needed it fast.

Maddy pulled open the first drawer, only to find office supplies, a stapler, paper clips, binder clips, and envelopes. The second drawer down was filled with blank DVDs, a spare set of keys, a package of Post-its (not big enough to write on), and a pair of sunglasses. The final drawer held colored construction paper, underneath which Maddy caught a glimpse of lined white paper. And underneath that . . . ? Maddy lifted out a leather-bound book, elegantly embossed with the phrase *Le Journal*.

Maddy blinked. Veronique's diary! What else could it be? Maddy glanced nervously toward the door. After all, searching for paper was one thing, but prying into another girl's diary was crossing a line. Would

Veronique herself suddenly appear all the way from America to curse her in French? Apparently not. All Maddy heard was the distant hum of traffic from the street below, mingled with the sounds of her mother rustling through the kitchen and Benji playing the final chord of the *Pathétique* Sonata. With the coast clear, she sat on the bed with the book. Again, she knew she shouldn't do it. But curiosity got the better of her. What did a girl who dressed and acted like Veronique Vadim think about? Besides, wasn't it a good opportunity to practice her French?

Yes, that's it! Her French! The perfect excuse, in case she was caught. Maddy stood and rifled quickly through her suitcase and found the ragged copy of her French/English dictionary. She then flopped on the bed, opened the book randomly to a page in the middle, and began to read.

le 17 Janvier

Stephan piend de nouveau toute la nuit. Je pense
qu'il est un génie.

Even as a C-minus student, Maddy got the gist of the meaning. To her delight, she didn't even need the dictionary. She glanced back across the courtyard to the adjacent apartment. Stephan—that was the boy's name. Clearly, Veronique had watched him paint all night. Even more, Veronique thought he was a *génie*, or genius. Maddy sighed, overcome by the romance of it. Underneath the tattoos and bad attitude, Veronique Vadim was as lovelorn as any normal teenage girl. In fact, maybe even more so. Had she really spent the entire night watching Stephan paint? Maybe that's why she had been in such a rotten mood—she had wanted to stay in Paris as badly as Maddy had wanted to stay in Chicago.

Excited, Maddy turned back to the diary. Now that she had taken the plunge, any guilt about invading another girl's privacy had vanished. She simply had to find out what she could about Veronique. She flipped to the next page—this was a longer entry, one that would take the dictionary to translate. But before Maddy had a chance to get started, a piercing cry echoed down the hall. Maddy sat up with a start. Had Veronique returned after all? Perhaps with a gang of French undercover agents, assigned to toss her into one of the dungeons of Versailles and throw away the key? But with the second scream, Maddy relaxed. She knew those vocal cords. It wasn't a Vadim or an agent. It was Benji. Hearing her parents' racing footsteps, Maddy crashed out the door and rushed behind. She looked down the hall just in time to see her mother disappear into another bedroom. Maddy followed.

A moment later Maddy found herself standing in the room of a three-year-old boy. A Thomas the Tank Engine mobile hung down from the ceiling. Above a small desk was a giant poster of Elmo. The tiny bed was shaped like the Batmobile.

Her brother was ranting.

"You expect me to stay in here? No wonder the Vadims didn't include pictures of Jean-Claude's bedroom online. The kid hasn't redecorated since he was two and a half!"

"Wow," Maddy said. The reason her brother had screamed was more than clear. "This is very weird."

"Weird?" Benji said. He was so upset his glasses had fogged. "All you can say is weird? A toddler's bed?" He looked at the wall. *"Le Elmo?"*

"This is a head-scratcher," Roger said. "Why does Jean-Claude have the room of a very little boy?"

Maddy saw a strange connection. "You know what else is strange? What do you think Veronique's room is like?"

"Easy," Rebecca said. "Heavy metal posters on the walls and a corpse in the closet."

"That's what I expected," Maddy said. "But the room isn't like that at all. It's actually nice. I even found her diary."

The minute the word was out of her mouth Maddy wished she could grab it out of the air and shove it back in. She knew exactly what her mother would say.

"What?" Rebecca said. "You were snooping?"

"Not snooping," Maddy said. "I found it when I was looking for a piece of paper."

"I assume you didn't read it?"

"You said you wanted us to cook. Don't tell me you weren't planning to use the Vadims' spices?"

"That's different," Rebecca said. "That's food, not private thoughts."

"It didn't say much anyway," Maddy said. "Veronique has a crush on this boy who lives across the way. He's a painter."

"Well, that's nice for Veronique," Benji said. "But let's not get off the subject. Check out this bed. I can live with it being shaped like the Batmobile. But how am I supposed to fit?"

It was a good question. Besides having Bert and Ernie sheets, it was almost too small for a toddler.

"It is a tad short," Roger said.

"Make that *really* short," Rebecca said.

"Who cares?" Maddy said. "Benji sleeps with you guys anyway."

"I guess that's what I'll keep on doing." But then Benji remembered the conversation with his sister on the plane. Maybe he should give his parents some time to themselves? "Or maybe I'll sleep in the living room."

His father seemed pleased.

"Sounds good, wingman."

Rebecca yawned. "Speaking of sleep, a short nap would do me a world of good right about now."

Roger's eyes went wide. "What? A nap? No, we have to stay up until eight-thirty tonight. That's the only way we're going to battle the jeg lag monster. That's the plan."

But Rebecca was already wandering sleepily toward the living room, with Maddy yawning at her heels. Rebecca spread out on a long blue sofa adjacent to the piano, and Maddy flopped back in an oversized easy chair.

"Sorry," Rebecca said. "New plan."

"No, we have to push through until tonight," Roger said. "Didn't you read my email?"

"Sorry, Dad," Maddy said. "Your emails go right into my spam folder."

"I read it," Benji said, following behind. "The key to

a successful travel experience is to stay awake the first day so that we can force ourselves onto European time. Was that it, Dad?"

"Exactly," Roger said. "So come on, people. I have a hundred and twenty-five dollars burning a hole in my pocket."

"Later, Roger," Rebecca said.

"No!" Roger said. He knew he was a pushover, but he'd be doomed if he'd let his family's sleep schedule get off on the very first day. "Come on, Hitchcocks! Off your lazy butts and move!"

CHAPTER SEVEN

That afternoon, Roger Hitchcock led his exhausted family on a tour of some of the most famous sights in Paris. First stop was the Centre Pompidou, one of the city's most impressive art centers. Next was Place des Vosges, a beautiful square planned over four hundred years ago by King Henry IV. All the while, Roger kept up a steady stream of commentary from his guidebook. Though Rebecca and the kids dragged their feet for the first couple of stops, by the time they reached the Arc de Triomphe, they had caught a second wind and begun to enjoy themselves. After a quick baguette and cheese from a sidewalk vendor, the family approached the Eiffel Tower.

"This tower was named after the architect who designed it, Gustave Eiffel," Roger said. "It was built in eighteen eighty-nine." He looked up. "It's one thousand sixty-three feet high."

Soon the family was riding a crowded elevator to the highest level. When the doors opened on the top, they spilled out to the viewing deck. Before them lay one of the most beautiful cities in the world, spread out like a picture postcard. There were the gardens of the Champs de Mars and the fountains of the Trocadero, mixed in with the elegant buildings of downtown Paris.

"Worth the trip, huh?" Roger said.

"You said it, Dad," Benji said.

Rebecca smiled. "It's stunning."

Maddy wandered down the observation deck, taking pictures with her phone. Benji saw his opening. Ever since they had landed in Paris, he had been waiting for the right moment to grill his sister again. Besides, why not let his parents enjoy the City of Lights alone for a moment?

"Later, guys," Benji called. With Maddy looking through the viewfinder of her camera, she was easy prey.

"Well," he said, coming up behind her. "I'm going on record with it."

Maddy remained focused on her picture. Though she hadn't wanted to admit it in front of her mother, the view was one of the most incredible things she had ever seen. She needed an image to send to Noah ASAP.

"With what?"

"They aren't getting a divorce."

Maddy squinted, snapped a picture of the Arc de Triomphe, then folded her phone. Then she sighed. Now was the time to nip the whole thing in the bud. She turned around to face her brother.

"Listen, Benji. I don't want to hurt you, but since you read my texts anyway, you might as well accept the truth. Mom and Dad are totally in their final stages."

Benji was undeterred. "Look!" he all but shouted, pointing wildly across the observation deck. "They're holding hands!"

It was true. There they stood, thirty or so feet away, hands clasped, taking in the view.

"That doesn't mean anything," Maddy said. "The last shards of a long-failed relationship."

Benji blinked. How could his sister ignore such obvious proof? "But how can you say that doesn't mean anything? Divorcing people don't hold hands. In fact, they probably don't even touch at all."

Maddy looked at her brother. Again, he was giving the champion puppy look—so cute she almost felt like patting him on the head. She hated to disappoint him. On the other hand, it wasn't her fault that he had read her texts.

"Listen," she said as gently as she could. "Here's how it went down. A few weeks ago, after school, I was downtown with Grace when I saw Mom enter this law firm Morganroth and Inker."

Benji blinked. "So?"

"Benji," Maddy said. "Morganroth and Inker handle divorces."

Benji felt himself tremble. "Divorces?" He had to stay clearheaded. This was no time to panic. "Are you sure that's all they do? Maybe they also do wills or sue people who steal baseball cards."

Yes, her brother was annoying, but why did he have to look at her like that? Breaking this news was even harder than she had imagined, almost like kicking a kitten.

"Sorry," she said. "I Googled them to make sure. Divorces. That's it."

Benji's lip was noticeably trembling. "No internet fraud?"

"Just divorce," Maddy said.

"That's not good," Benji said. "That's not good!"

"Right," Maddy said. "Why else would Mom have gone there if not to check out how to dump Dad? And listen."

"Yeah?"

Maddy paused. She hated to do it, but there was something else she simply had to say. "When they do break up, don't feel we have to do this 'you and me always being together' thing. One weekend you can go to Dad's, the next weekend I can go to Dad's."

Benji felt as though he had taken a punch to the stomach. It was bad enough to hear that his mother had consulted a divorce lawyer. Was he about to lose his parents and his only sibling?

"What? Are you . . . *breaking* up with me?"

Maddy met her brother's eyes. Tears were certainly on the way. She didn't want to hurt him, but she needed her space. Wasn't it better to get it all out now?

"I'm just saying that I want time apart," Maddy said. "No offense, OK? You're still my brother. No big deal."

A lone tear formed in the corner of Benji's right eye and rolled slowly down his cheek. "Why are you being so mean?"

"I'm not being mean, Benji. Just honest. Hey, don't cry. Don't do it. Come on. We're in Paris. Don't freak out on me."

With that, Maddy looked over her shoulder to see if she could pass Benji off to her mother. Even from a distance she could see that her mom looked noticeably pale. Maddy didn't think much of it at first—her mom's middle name was practically "motion sickness"—but then the situation got dicier. Just like that, her mother swooned. Her father made a move to catch her but missed. Then, suddenly, a sturdy man with a cleft in his chin so distinct that Maddy could see it from all the way across the top of the tower swooped in from out of nowhere and grabbed Rebecca before she hit the pavement.

"Come on!" Maddy said.

In seconds, she and Benji were at their parents' side. The man with the chin was now holding Rebecca firmly in his arms.

"Oh my gosh," she was saying. "One look over the edge . . . I guess I've never been this high before."

"No worries," the man said. He had a deep voice and an American accent. "It happens all the time up here."

Benji looked to his dad, suddenly extremely concerned. Maybe Maddy was right, after all. They had been in Paris for less than a day and some handsome guy with a movie-star chin was already horning in on his mom?

"That's OK, sir," Benji said. "My dad has got it from here."

Roger looked relieved to have some backup, even from a nine-year-old boy. "Righto. I've got it."

But when the man passed Rebecca over to Roger, he realized that it had been a long time since their last fireman's carry. He stumbled backward against the rail.

"Roger!" Rebecca called.

Once again, the stranger was there.

"Allow me."

"No," Roger said. "I've got it!"

This time Roger slipped and dropped his wife to the observation deck floor. The man was ready to pinch-hit, of course. In moments, he had Rebecca settled on a bench with a bottle of water.

"Thank you so much," Rebecca said. Though flushed, her interest in the man could not have been more obvious to Benji. Suddenly everything Maddy had told him seemed one hundred percent true.

"You're American, too?" Rebecca asked him.

The man smiled. To go with his stunning chin, he

had movie-star teeth—white, straight, and winning. It was a beautiful smile, but almost too beautiful. Benji didn't know if he had ever trusted someone less.

"Actually from Des Moines. The name's Harry Huberman."

"Nice to meet you, Huberman," Roger said. "We'll take it from here."

"No, no. You must let my driver take you back to your hotel."

Rebecca's eyes lit up. "Driver? You have a driver?" She looked up at Roger. "Did you hear that? He has a driver."

"I heard," Roger said.

"Not my own," Huberman said with a self-deprecating chuckle. "I work for the embassy."

"How impressive." She put out her hand. Benji saw her smile warmly, the way she used to smile at his father. "Rebecca Hitchcock."

"I'm the husband," Roger said. "Roger."

Huberman took Rebecca's hand. "Nice to meet you." He turned to Maddy and Benji. "And these are your charming children?"

"Yes," Rebecca said. "Maddy and Benji."

Benji hadn't ever remembered feeling so uncomfortable or seeing his father look so miserable.

"Thanks again for your help," Roger said. "We have it from here."

But Rebecca wasn't finished. "What do you do for the embassy?"

The man reached into his suit jacket and took out a card. "Diplomatic corps. We host parties, mostly. But if you ever need anything in Paris—a doctor, a restaurant reservation—just call, OK? I've lived here for seventeen years."

Benji hated the look in his mother's eyes. He was suddenly convinced that she liked this guy. It was all he could do not to kick him in the shins. Or push him off the tower.

"Well, thanks, much."

"Please. Allow my driver to take you home."

"That's OK," Roger said. "We've got it. We'll take a cab."

"A taxi?" Rebecca said. "Do you know how much that costs?"

Roger smiled. "Let the good times roll, dear. We're on vacation. Come on. Let's go, Hitchcocks." He looked at the man again. "Nice to meet you."

"Likewise," Huberman said. "Don't forget to call if you need anything."

Moments later, the family was on the elevator going

down. Benji saw Maddy shoot him a knowing glance. Benji stared blankly ahead, too shaken to respond.

"What a charming man," Rebecca said.

No one answered. On ground level, Roger quickly flagged a cab. Benji walked slowly, ten feet behind the rest of his family, head down, the joy of the day suddenly squeezed dry.

"Come on, sport," Roger called, obviously trying to remain upbeat. "Our chariot awaits."

With a sigh, Benji quickened his pace. But then he stopped short. Could it be? Suddenly thoughts of his parents' potential marital problems were replaced by a more immediate fear. Crouching behind a lamppost was the Elevator Man, his pierced eyebrow glinting in the afternoon sun. Worse, he was pointing a camera straight at the family—taking pictures! Heart thumping, Benji turned to his family.

"It's him," he whispered.

"What?" Maddy said.

"The Elevator Man!"

"*Who?*" Roger asked.

"From the building. I could've sworn he was looking at us funny when we went up to the apartment. Look!"

Benji pointed. "There!"

But what was this? The Elevator Man was gone. Instead, a young girl was helping an elderly lady into a cab. Benji looked around, breathless and confused. His mother placed a hand on his shoulder.

"Sweetie, you've been reading too many spy novels."

"I don't read spy novels, Mom," Benji said. "The Elevator Man from the building was following us— snapping pictures."

"OK, fine," Maddy said. "But where is he then?"

Benji wheeled around, surveying the entire area. He felt the blood rush from his face. Was he seeing things? The Elevator Man had been standing by a lamp-post. Now he was gone. But didn't international spies appear and disappear like magic?

"It's been a long, long day, sport. Come on. In the cab."

"Dad. He was there!"

"Well, he's gone now. Let's go home."

"Wait!"

He was many things, but crazy wasn't one of them. Why was the Elevator Man following them? What did he want? Worse, why didn't his family believe him?

Benji took a final desperate look. Nothing. Only then did he let his father lead him to the taxi.

CHAPTER EIGHT

Not only couldn't Roger Hitchcock stop his wife from swooning into the arms of an attractive stranger, but he soon discovered that he was powerless in the face of an even more cunning opponent: the jet lag monster. After an early dinner at a corner bistro, the family stumbled back to the Vadims' with one thing on their collective minds: sleep.

"I am wiped," Maddy said, and flopped, spread-eagled, facedown on the sofa.

"Me, too," Rebecca said. "Catch ya later."

She craned her neck and yawned, stumbling blindly

toward the Vadims' master bedroom.

To Roger's horror, even Benji's eyes were closing. "Off to the Batmobile. Even if it's too small," he murmured. "Need. Shut. Eye."

"But it's only six-thirty," Roger said. "We have to stay up at least another two hours."

It was too late. As he lurched toward the sofa to shake Maddy awake, Roger was stopped cold by a yawn of his own. A weariness enveloped him like a warm bath. Wandering blindly into his own room, he fell asleep next to his wife. Even on vacation, Roger and Rebecca slept back-to-back.

Exhausted, the Hitchcocks remained dead to the world all the way through the night and into midmorning. In fact, the family might have slept straight on through until noon had it not been for a series of insistent raps on the door around ten. Roger stirred first. Still clothed, he roused himself from bed and lurched to the foyer.

"Monsieur Vadim?" a voice said. "Monsieur Vadim!"

Roger scratched his head and reached for the door. To his surprise, standing before him was a messenger in a blue coat and cap.

"Um . . . *oui?*"

The messenger handed him an envelope. *"Pour vous, monsieur."*

Roger took the envelope, and the messenger retreated back down the stairs.

"What's that?"

Roger looked over his shoulder. It was Benji, clothes rumpled and glasses off. Clearly, he had just woken up, too. Without waiting for an answer, the boy grabbed the envelope and ripped it open.

"Hmmm, tickets. Four of 'em." He held one close to his eyes and squinted. "For tonight, too. *L'opéra.*"

"An opera?" Roger said. He laughed. "I'm sort of embarrassed to admit this, but I've never been to one."

"Well here's our chance, Dad." Then Benji had a thought. He sidled closer to his father. "And you know what? I hear operas are, you know . . . "

"What, buddy?"

"Well, romantic."

Roger grinned. "Romantic, huh?"

"Yeah."

Despite his sister's so-called proof, Benji still hadn't given up on getting his parents back on track. The way he saw it, his father just needed to be a little more proactive. Benji didn't know much, but he had seen plenty of men woo plenty of women on TV.

"So here's what you do, OK? I hear that people bring bottles of wine to the opera in Paris. So you sneak in a bottle. I'll help you with that. Then, during the first big aria, you pour her a glass, right? Then you whisper something soft and sweet like, 'To a lady more beautiful than the most stunning monuments of Europe.'"

Roger gave his son a funny look.

"Have you been reading romance novels?"

Benji shook his head. "No, Dad. I just think it could be a fun way to spice things up tonight."

"What's tonight?"

It was Maddy, entering with a towel wrapped around her body and another wrapped around her head. She had been so tired she hadn't even had time to get back into Veronique's diary.

"Yo, Sis!" Benji said. "We're going to the opera!"

"The opera?" She shrugged. "Cool, I guess."

"So what's the etiquette on this anyway?" Roger asked. "Do we call the Vadims in Chicago to see if it's OK?"

"Why?" Maddy said. "They can't use them."

"Use what?"

Now Rebecca entered, wearing a nightgown.

"Opera tickets, Mom!" Benji said. "A messenger dropped them off for the Vadims."

Rebecca frowned. "Well, if they aren't ours, we can't use them."

Roger felt a flash of irritation. Why did his wife always take the dim view of things? Yes, he had wondered if they should call the Vadims for permission, but after the little pep talk from Benji, he had never really considered not going.

"Of course we use them. The vacation gods are smiling!"

"They're free, Mom," Maddy said. "Dad's favorite price."

"But what if the seats are with the Vadims' friends?" Rebecca asked.

"We'll wow them with our French," Roger said.

"Then what about clothes?"

"Rebecca!" Roger said. "Look around. The Vadims live like kings. Their closets are swimming with high-class duds. What we borrow and return won't hurt them."

And so it was decided. And once Rebecca accepted the unexpected gift, the trip took a turn for the better. Looking forward to a night on the town, the family rallied. That afternoon, they walked through Saint-Germain-des-Prés, toured Notre Dame, and visited the Rodin Museum. For dinner, Roger splurged at a

local restaurant, where Maddy surprised everyone—
and herself—by ordering her main course in French.

"See what you can do if you apply yourself?"
Rebecca said.

When Maddy saw her mother grin, she allowed
herself a half smile in return.

Then, on the way home before the opera, Roger
snuck into a liquor store and bought a bottle of what
the shopkeeper called *un Merlot très excellent*. Strolling
across the Seine, Benji sidled up to his father.

"You got the wine?"

Roger patted the package. "I do."

"Glasses?"

"I'll take two from the Vadims'."

"Bottle opener?"

Roger scowled. He had forgotten. What would he
do? Break the bottle over the seat?

"No worries, Dad," Benji said. "I've got your back."

He reached into his pocket and handed his father a
corkscrew.

"Thanks, wingman."

"I'm on it, Dad. By the way, sorry to be so freaked
yesterday afternoon about that elevator guy. Must have
been the jet lag. It's astonishing how sleep deprivation
can affect the human mind. I read a study."

"Don't worry about it, sport. We've all been a bit stressed lately."

"Hey, you two," Rebecca shouted from the other side of the bridge. "Hurry up! It's almost dress-up time!"

Benji smiled. Over the course of the day, things had seemed to warm up between his parents. Then it got better. The moment the family pushed through the front door to the Vadim apartment, Rebecca all but sprinted down the hall to Beatrix Vadim's immense closets. Roger ran behind. Best yet, they were both laughing.

"I've been waiting for this all day," Rebecca said.

"Me, too!"

Looking down the hall, Benji saw his father do something he hadn't attempted in years: the fireman's carry! He lifted Rebecca into the air and spun her around the room.

Benji turned excitedly to his sister. "Hey, Maddy!"

"What?" she said. She had run for her room, too, hoping to catch a few minutes with Veronique's diary before leaving for the theater.

"Mads!" Benji called again. "Check this out!"

"This better be good," Maddy whispered to herself.

It was, but not for the reason Benji had hoped. The

minute Maddy and Benji got down the hall to their parents' room, they saw Roger catch his foot on the carpet. Stepping onto the hardwood floor, he slipped, then fell.

"Roger!" Rebecca called.

"Dad!" Benji cried.

Thankfully, Rebecca landed on the bed. As for Roger, he hit the floor hard on his rear end.

"Ouch," Maddy said. "Nice one, Dad."

Rebecca smiled. "Either I'm heavier than I used to be or you're out of shape."

Roger forced a laugh. "Just out of shape, sweets."

Benji looked from his parents to his sister. Maddy met his eyes with a sad shrug. She had been happy to see her father trying to rekindle the old spark, but it felt like too little too late.

"So what now?" Benji said.

Never one to admit defeat, Roger rose promptly to his feet and helped Rebecca off the bed.

"What next?" he said. "Dress-up time."

By the time the family Hitchcock stepped onto the street a short time later, they were utterly transformed. Rebecca was in one of Beatrix Vadim's most elegant gowns, a blue velvet. Roger was wearing one of Xavier

Vadim's tuxedos as though it had been custom made just for him, along with a light overcoat large enough to hide the bottle of wine and glasses in the interior pockets. Maddy had searched through Veronique's closets and found a trim-fitting black dress and red heels, while Benji strutted down the sidewalk in a black beret and a black cape.

Maddy laughed. "I can't believe you really wore a Batman cape."

"My options were limited, OK? I'm sharing rooms with a three-year-old, remember?"

"Quiet," Rebecca said with a smile. "Benji looks very handsome."

The boy blushed. He was used to receiving compliments about his brains, not his looks.

"Oh, whatever," he said, but then caught his reflection in a storefront window and tipped his beret at a jaunty angle. Handsome? Why not.

"Taxi!" Roger called.

It was a quick trip through the city to the opera house. And when the family got out of the cab, a good day got even better. The Paris Opera was performed in a building that more closely resembled a palace than a theater.

"Oh my lord," Rebecca said. "I had no idea."

"This thing took over twenty years to build," Benji said. "The architect was a guy named Charles Garnier."

"How do you know that?" Maddy asked.

"I snuck into an internet café and Googled it."

"You would," Maddy said with a sigh.

"It's also got seventeen floors," Benji went on.

Rebecca waved toward the doors. "Then we better get going. It might take us a while to find our seats."

The family moved across a wide open plaza toward the entrance. By that point, Benji had put aside all thoughts of the Elevator Man. Roger had forgotten about Harry Huberman. Rebecca had blocked out the memory of their long trip. For the time being, Maddy had even forgotten about Veronique's diary.

By the standards of a typical overworked, stressed-out American family, the Hitchcocks were relaxed. Enjoying each other's company, they had no idea whatsoever that they were being watched—and not by the Elevator Man. As the family made their way into the thick of the crowd, an unusually tall man in a light yellow suit with an orange tie stepped out from behind a street vendor, enjoying the final bites of a baguette. When the Hitchcocks disappeared inside the building, the man wiped his mouth with a handkerchief and followed. A moment later he slipped behind a column and watched the Hitchcocks admire the lavish lobby, an absolutely enormous space complete with a sweeping marble stairway, elaborately carved columns that rose to the ceiling, and chandeliers that blazed like burning torches.

"My gosh," Rebecca said. "The inside is even more stunning than the outside."

Roger grinned. All that mattered to him was that his wife was happy. Suddenly a house swap to Paris seemed like a stroke of rare genius.

"*Ah, oui,*" the usher said, taking Roger's tickets. "*En haut d'escalier e tournez-vous à droite.*"

"What did he say?" Rebecca whispered to Maddy.

"I think we go up and right."

Maddy was correct. As the family ascended the wide-open staircase, the tall stranger gave his own ticket to the usher and followed behind, close enough not to lose track but far enough away not to be seen. At the top of the stairs, the man watched another usher show the Hitchcocks through a door shrouded with red velvet curtains. He then went to the bar for a drink. He'd bide his time for a while.

Inside the curtains, the Hitchcocks found themselves in a box that held four seats. Directly below lay the orchestra section. Straight ahead was the stage, now covered by a blue curtain.

"What seats!" Rebecca said.

While his wife was focused on the spectacle around her, Roger carefully slipped the wine, glasses, and corkscrew out of his coat and placed them under his seat. He then screwed up his courage and slipped his arm around his wife's waist.

"This is the Paris I promised you."

She squeezed his hand. "This is so much better than decent."

"*La Bohème* is by Puccini," Benji told his sister as she took her seat beside him. "It's the most performed opera in the world."

Maddy smiled. "Please don't tell me you're going to pepper me with opera facts for the rest of the night."

"I was considering it."

"De-consider it, OK?"

The children continued to bicker, but Roger and Rebecca were too caught up in the splendor of the evening to intercede. Their focus was on the stage. Soon enough, the chandelier dimmed, the curtain opened, and the show began. Though never an opera fan in particular, Roger found himself being swept up by the music. But what mattered more was Rebecca. During the first act, Roger spent as much time looking at her as at the stage. Every time she smiled, he felt vindi-cated. And then, the pièce de résistance. During a loud orchestral passage, Roger quietly opened the bottle of wine. As the cork popped out, Benji held out the glasses. Roger poured.

"Thanks, wingman," he whispered, then turned to his wife. "May I offer you a fine Merlot?"

Roger didn't recall her ever being so surprised—not even when he had proposed. A look of pure joy lit up her face. Roger poured his own glass and put the bottle down at his side.

"Nice, Daddy-o," Benji whispered.

Benji smiled as he watched his parents hold hands again. Everything seemed perfect. Benji was going to prod his sister to show her what was happening a row ahead, but she had fallen asleep. For his part, Benji was enthralled by the opera. Never before had he heard so many beautiful voices sing together in such perfect harmony with such a stirring orchestra. He wasn't sure of the plot, but men and women were declaring undying love. And at the end, so he heard, someone died. Not bad.

In fact, Benji was so engrossed in the opera that he didn't hear the man in the yellow suit and orange tie enter their box and clear his throat. Clearly, his father hadn't either. When the man tapped him on the shoulder, he said, "Quiet, sport. It's almost intermission."

Benji swallowed hard. The man in the suit was leaning over him now, whispering to his father.

"*Bonjour, Monsieur.*"

Roger looked up, then exchanged a glance with Benji. Who was this man? Benji immediately thought he was an usher coming to throw them out for stealing tickets.

"Xavier Vadim?" the man went on.

Benji felt his heart begin to thump in perfect rhythm with the fast-paced music onstage. Would his father tell the truth?

"Uh, yes?" he said. "I mean, uh, *oui.*"

"*Venez avec moi. Allons-y.*"

The man stood. He motioned toward the door. Roger looked at Rebecca.

"What's going on?" his wife asked.

"Not sure," Roger said nervously. "I'll handle it."

"Are we in trouble?" Benji asked.

Roger forced a smile. "Of course not. Leave it to me. It's all good."

Benji watched his father follow the man through the curtains to the upper lobby. If he were an usher, maybe his dad could offer him a little money to look the other way? Benji knew he shouldn't listen in, but this was too strange to sit out. Besides, hadn't Maddy already looked in Veronique's diary? Why should she get all the fun? With his sister asleep and his mother already focused back on the stage, Benji slipped quietly out of the box. Through the curtain he could see his father and the man standing ten feet away in the upper lobby by the stairway.

"Listen," Roger was saying. He was wearing his most ingratiating smile. "I think there's been a mis-understanding."

To Benji's dismay, the man was all business.

"*L'avion attend*," he said.

Roger blinked. "Um . . . excuse . . . *moi?*"

The man leaned close. Benji could sense his father's fear.

"*Est-ce que c'est votre famille?*"

Roger painted on a fake smile. "I'm sorry, but your accent's a little thick. If this is about the seats, I can explain everything." He paused. "Maybe if you try English?"

"Not the seats," the man said with a heavy French accent. "The airplane awaits." The man paused, studying Roger's face. "The flight to Algiers." Now he glanced toward the door to the box seats. "Where is your baggage?"

Benji gasped. The man was in league with the Elevator Man! He had to be! And he was about to kidnap his father and take him to Algiers! But what could Benji do about it? Call for an usher? The police?

But if Benji was panicked, his father seemed almost relieved.

"I'm sorry," Roger said. "Flight to Algiers? I think you have me mixed up with someone else."

Yes, Benji thought. That's it. A case of mistaken identity. His father would clear things up and everything would be fine.

"*Oui*," the man whispered intensely. "As you requested."

Inside the theater, Benji heard the soprano and tenor hold a high, loud note. When they finished, the audience cheered.

"Like I said, we've had a misunderstanding."

He turned toward the box. The man grabbed his arm hard.

"Are you saying you aren't honoring your agreement, Monsieur Vadim?"

Benji's brief reprieve was over. Suddenly there was an intensity to the man's tone that told him that his family had blundered into something serious.

Roger swallowed, but his throat was bone dry. "You

see, I'm not Xavier Vadim. I'm Roger Hitchcock!"

Another burst of applause came from inside the theater. Benji could hear shouts of "Bravo!" echo into the lobby.

"I guess it's intermission," his father said.

The man moved closer. His voice now held no traces of politeness. "Do not play games with me, Vadim! Where is the MGF?"

Benji felt his legs go weak. He clutched the curtain for support.

"The MGF?" his father said.

"You heard me!"

"I don't know anything about it!"

"We had a deal! You tell me! Now!"

Roger pulled himself free. When the man lunged for him again, Benji broke out of the curtain and pushed the man away—hard. To his surprise, the man's foot caught on the carpet. The next thing Benji knew, the man was falling backward, head-over-heels, down a marble stairway like a giant yellow Gumby. Father and son stood frozen, watching the man somersault down, down, down all the way to the bottom, where he landed on his back with a loud thud.

"What were you doing there?" Roger asked.

"I was curious," Benji said.

A split second later, the Hitchcock men became aware that intermission had started. The lobby was filling quickly and the man, though shaken, was rising slowly to his feet.

"We're out of here!" Roger said.

Benji pushed his way back through the growing crowd to his box, where Rebecca was standing up, still looking happily at the stage. Maddy was awake now, glancing sleepily through the program.

"Wasn't that beautiful?" Rebecca asked.

Benji looked at his dad. Best to let him explain things. Roger took a deep breath and tried to appear calm.

"Did I see a man in a yellow suit?" Maddy asked. "Or was I dreaming?"

"Funny story," Roger said with a forced grin. "We never got to exchange names. But you know what? I think these opera tickets may not have been our single greatest idea."

Rebecca blinked. "What?"

"Come on, honey. Time to go."

Rebecca looked stricken. "Oh, Roger! I have to see what happens."

"Sorry! We're leaving."

"But it's only intermission!" Rebecca said. "There

are three more acts! We haven't finished the wine!"

"Mom!" Benji said. "This is serious!"

Roger did something he almost never did—raised his voice. "Rebecca! Now!"

When Benji followed his family out of the box, he expected the man to be waiting, possibly with a gun. To the boy's relief, he was still struggling up the steps against a great tide of operagoers headed downstairs to the bar and bathrooms.

"This way!" Roger called, and all but yanked Maddy across the lobby, away from the stairs.

"Roger?" Rebecca said. "What's happening? Benji? Do you know anything?"

"We'll tell you when we're safe," Roger said.

Benji looked over his shoulder. The man was a step away from the top of the stairs and was scanning the crowd.

"Over here!" Benji said, and pushed his family against a wall, out of the man's line of vision.

Roger turned to his daughter. "Maddy. What's the French word for fire exit?"

"*Sortie!*" Maddy pointed. "Right there!"

A moment later the family was running full out across the lobby. They ducked through the exit and all but galloped down the stairs and out of the opera house.

With every step, Benji expected to hear the man's footsteps—maybe even a gunshot. But in moments they were safely in a cab. As the driver moved from the curb, Benji glanced out the back window. There was no one following. They had escaped—for now.

But from who?

CHAPTER NINE

Back at the Vadims', the family hustled upstairs as fast as they could.

"I still don't get it," Rebecca said when they were finally inside the apartment and had changed back into their regular clothes. "It's not like we did anything wrong. The Vadims couldn't use the tickets. They're in Chicago, for crying out loud."

"I know," Roger said. "But this guy thought Monsieur Vadim was headed to Algiers."

"Algiers?" Maddy said.

"Yeah," Benji said. "He was looking for the MGF."

"What's that?" Rebecca asked.

"We don't know, Mom," Benji said. "Or if this Algerian guy has any connection to the Elevator Man."

"Forget the Elevator Man," Rebecca said. "We should call that man from the embassy, Harry Huberman— that's what we should do."

"And say what?" Roger said. "That a strange guy in a yellow suit accosted me at the opera, so my son tossed him down the stairs?"

Maddy looked disbelievingly at Benji. "I still can't believe you did that."

"Oh, believe," Benji said. "Right, Daddy-o?"

"Right, wingman."

"But wait," Rebecca said. "Who was the guy anyway? You still haven't said."

"That's the point, Mom," Benji said. "We don't know."

Before Rebecca could respond, there were three loud raps at the front door. The family froze. For a second that felt like a minute, everyone was silent.

"It's him!" Benji whispered finally. "The Algerian."

"Has he come for the MLF?" Maddy asked.

"MGF," Benji said.

"Whatever."

"No one move," Roger said. "Act like we aren't here

and whoever it is will go away."

Again the family was quiet, doing their best to draw courage from one another. When three more knocks filled the room, Roger broke first.

"It's him. It has to be!"

"What do we do?" Benji asked. "Want me to push him down another flight of stairs?"

"You'll do no such thing!" Rebecca said.

But then a voice came from the other side of the door. Not of a man but of a girl speaking heavily accented English.

"I know you are in there! I saw the lights from the street."

Roger hadn't ever remembered feeling so relieved.

"I'm sorry?" Rebecca called out, walking to the door. "Who is it, please?"

"Camille," the voice said. *"L'amie de Veronique."*

"Veronique's friend," Maddy said. "We're safe."

Roger and Benji slapped five.

"Yes!" Benji said. "Safe!"

"Show her in, sweets," Roger said.

Rebecca pulled open the door, revealing a short, stocky girl whose twisted expression brought to mind an irate pitbull. She was dressed entirely in black.

"Can we help you?" Rebecca asked.

Without a word, the girl marched toward Veronique's room, throwing a hard shoulder into Rebecca as she passed.

"*Excusez-moi!*" Roger cried. "That's my wife!"

Then Camille was in Veronique's room. The other Hitchcocks hurried behind, with Maddy at the lead.

"Hey, watch my stuff," she said.

"I am not looking for your stuff," Camille said, and went straight to the desk, opened the third drawer, and began to root under the paper.

"Hey, hey," Roger said. "This is a little bit out of the ordinary."

Camille threw all the paper on the floor.

"Where is it?" she called out.

Maddy swallowed hard. "Where is what?"

Camille took a step toward her. Though not much taller than Benji, she looked as though she could knock Maddy out with one hand.

"Don't lie to me. I can tell in your eyes that you have it."

Despite ongoing battles with her mother, Maddy didn't think of herself as a fighter. With peers, she was more likely to back down than make a stand. Then again, she had never met anyone as pugnacious as Camille. True, Maddy had accidentally stumbled on the diary. She had even read a page or two. But why should she hand it over to a warthog of a girl who barged into the Vadims' home like she owned it without so much as a smile? Besides, there was something else: Why had Camille shown up at the Vadims' right after the strange scare at the opera? Was there was some sort of connection?

Maddy met the girl's eyes. "I have no idea what you're talking about."

Camille took another step toward Maddy. The two girls were practically touching.

"You are lying!" Camille said to Maddy.

Maddy didn't budge. "Don't you have an appointment somewhere?"

"Are you asking me to leave?"

"I'm telling you to leave!"

"No one talks to Camille like that!"

The short girl lowered her head like a ram and lunged. Maddy jumped aside a split second before Camille connected with her gut. Then Roger stepped in, waving his arms.

"OK, easy does it! No fighting on my watch." He turned to Camille. "My daughter doesn't know what you're saying. She barely speaks French. She got a C-minus."

Maddy had never been happier about getting a bad

grade. Camille nudged Roger aside and held Maddy's gaze.

"*Je retournerai*," she said. "I will call Veronique and *je retournerai* very soon."

The French girl stalked out of the apartment, slamming the door behind her. The moment the coast was clear, Rebecca turned to Maddy.

"What in the world was that about?"

"She wanted Veronique's diary."

"Then why didn't you give it to her?"

"I didn't like her," Maddy said. "I also have a feeling— a strong feeling—that Veronique's diary holds some sort of a clue."

"A clue?" Roger asked.

Benji rubbed his hands together. "Ooh, I like this! The plot thickens!"

"No, it doesn't," Rebecca said. "This is crazy."

"Is it?" Maddy said. "You think it's a coincidence that someone tried to put Dad on a plane to Algiers and the minute we get home a strange girl barges in looking for Veronique's diary?"

Roger nodded. "Maddy," he said. "Get the diary!"

Moments later the Hitchcock family was gathered around the kitchen table. Maddy held the diary while

Benji manned the *French/English Dictionary*. Roger had a pad and paper. As for Rebecca, she paced nervously, watching over everyone.

"Are you sure we should be doing this?" she asked.

"Absolutely," Roger said. "Camille wanted the diary for a reason. It might hold some sort of secret about this family. We need to figure out what's going on."

With Benji helping her translate, Maddy was able to get a reasonably quick sense of what most of Veronique's entries entailed. Many were about Stephan, the boy across the courtyard who she adored. The rest were less interesting, mostly random observations about school or her parents. "All normal stuff," as Benji put it. But then, after about a half an hour of steady work, Maddy and Benji came upon a new subject. In red Magic Marker, Veronique had written: *"Je deteste Sofia!!!"*

"Sofia?" Roger said. "Who's that?"

"And why does she hate her?" Rebecca asked.

No one knew. But a page later, Veronique brought her up again, this time writing in all caps: *"JE SOU-HAITE QUE SOFIA N'AIT PAS FAIT EXIST!!!"*

"She wishes Sofia didn't exist?" Maddy said.

"Whoa," Benji said. "That's pretty extreme."

"Maybe Xavier Vadim has a girlfriend named Sofia,"

Rebecca said. "Maybe he's planning to leave the family. Maybe that's what this is all about."

"Who knows?" Maddy said. She turned to the next page of the diary. "OK, wait a second. I think I have something. *Mon père est voleur.* My father is a . . . come on, Benj, help me out."

Benji was already flipping through the dictionary. "*Voleur.* Wait for it. Hold on. Got it! *Thief.*"

"My God," Rebecca said, eyes wide. "Is Veronique saying her dad is a crook?"

"Could be," Roger said.

"It gets better," Maddy said. "Listen up. Veronique writes that she found some sort of a *fiole.* What's that, Benji?"

"Wait for it," he said, leafing through the book. "A *fiole* is . . . a vial!"

"Vile?" Maddy said. "Like in disgusting?"

"No," Benji said. "A vial, like in chemistry."

"Chemistry professors use vials," Roger said. "And Vadim is a chemistry professor."

"So let's back up," Rebecca said. "What do we have so far?"

Maddy looked at her translation. "Veronique discovered that her father stole a vial, which she saw in his . . . *cachette.*"

Again, Benji flipped through the dictionary at lightning speed. "Hmmm . . . *cachette* . . . that means . . . secret hiding place!"

"Secret hiding place?" Maddy said.

"This is getting creepier and creepier," Rebecca said.

Roger paced the table, sorting it all out. "So according to Veronique, her father stole some sort of a vial and has it tucked away in a secret hiding place. But that could be anywhere."

"Maybe we can figure out where it is," Benji said. "Dad? Where's your secret hiding place?"

"Everyone knows that," Maddy said. "The drawer by his bed."

"Have you been stealing twenty-dollar bills from your father?"

Maddy rolled her eyes. "Of course, Mom. How else would I survive?"

"Ladies!" Roger shouted. "Please! Let's focus on the situation at hand. We've got to find this secret hiding place. Now work with me. And think like a Vadim! Get looking!"

With those words, the family dispersed through the apartment like mice scurrying through a maze. Maddy made a beeline for the master bath, where she searched the medicine cabinets and shower. Rebecca combed through the master closet, patting down Beatrix Vadim's dresses and searching in each one of her shoes. While the ladies of the family were busy in the Vadims' bedroom, Roger searched the living room, looking inside the grand piano and under sofas.

It was Benji, however—the family member who hung close to the kitchen—who found what they were looking for. The clue wasn't in a secret hiding place but in plain sight. On the countertop was a piece of scrap paper. On it was the vague outline of some writing. Benji held it up to the light.

"Hey, guys!" he shouted. "*Guys!*"

But an even louder shout filled the apartment.

"Oh, yes! *Yes!*"

His mom. She ran into the kitchen, clutching a wad of bills.

"What's that?" Benji asked.

"I found it in one of Beatrix Vadim's high heels," Rebecca said. "It must be her mad money."

"Mad money?" Benji asked.

"Money a wife stores away in case she wants to make a quick dash to freedom," Rebecca said.

Benji's eyes went wide. How did his mother know so much about a woman trying to leave her husband?

He turned to Maddy, who had "I told you so" written all over her face.

"Nice find, Rebecca," Roger said, entering the room. "How much is there?"

"Nine thousand Euros!"

"Hey," Benji said. "Forget about the mad money, OK?" He reached for two pots on the stove and banged them over his head. *"I found something, people! A real clue!"*

He held up the piece of scrap paper. Roger squinted. "It's a blank piece of paper."

"No, no," Benji said. He plopped the pots back on the stove. "Look more closely. See there? There are the outlines of a name and number, as though someone wrote on a piece of paper that used to be on top of it."

"That could be," Rebecca said. "But I can't read it."

"Leave this to me," Maddy said.

A moment later she was rifling through Beatrix Vadim's spice collection.

"Maddy?" her mother said. "What in the world are you looking for?"

"This!"

Maddy grabbed a red bottle.

"Paprika?" Roger said.

Without saying a word, Maddy laid the notepaper

carefully on the countertop, then sprinkled the red paprika over it.

"What are you doing?" Roger asked. "Seasoning the paper?"

"Something like that."

As the spice settled on the paper, the outlines of the indented word and numbers became clearer.

"How'd you learn to do that?" Rebecca asked.

"Grace showed me."

"Why?"

Maddy smiled. "You don't want to know."

Roger took the paper and held it up to the light.

"Check this out, people! Our first clue!"

There in vivid relief was a simple word: SOFIA. Underneath was what appeared to be a telephone number: 07-08-124-977.

CHAPTER TEN

"Sofia!" Rebecca said. "Just like in the diary!"

"Now we're getting somewhere," Roger said.

Benji grabbed the phone. "I'm calling right now."

"Wait," Maddy said. "It's eleven-thirty at night."

"Haven't you ever heard of the element of surprise?" Benji said. "The old EOS."

He held up the paper and quickly dialed. The family huddled close.

"Well?" Rebecca said.

"Shh!" Benji said. "It's ringing!"

"What are you going to say?" Maddy asked.

"Duh? I'll ask for Sofia."

"What if she doesn't speak English?"

"I'll fake it."

"Oh, big man. This I gotta see."

"Quiet, Maddy," Rebecca said. "Let your brother concentrate."

Benji was already putting down the receiver.

"What's wrong?" Roger asked.

"No answer."

"You sure?" Maddy said.

"Of course I'm sure. No one picked up."

"But did you let it ring long enough?"

"Sure I did."

"I don't think so."

Rebecca waved her arms. "Shhh, the two of you. There was no answer, OK?"

Benji folded the paprika-covered note and slipped it into his back pocket. "We might need this later."

"Good thinking," Roger said.

"So what next?" Rebecca asked.

The phone rang.

The Hitchcocks froze. Ever since meeting up with the Algerian at the opera, they had known that they had stumbled into something—possibly even something big. At the same time, their adventures had seemed vaguely unreal, almost as though they were happening to some other family. But now the ringing phone woke them to the seriousness of their situation. Clearly, Benji's phone call had reached someone. And now that person was calling back. Would he be angry? Did he know the tall man Benji had pushed down the stairs? Or the Elevator Man? Did he, too, want Veronique's diary?

"I'm scared," Maddy said.

"I'll second that," Benji said.

"Don't answer," Rebecca said.

The phone rang again.

Roger knew the risks. If he was smart, he would gather his family, take a cab straight to the airport, and jump on the next plane home. But this was one of those moments when curiosity trumped common sense. Yes, Roger knew he should run—and run fast. But he was in too deep to turn away.

He picked up on the third ring.

"Vadim résidence," he said in his best French accent.

"Roger Hitchcock?"

Roger almost shook with relief.

"It's Xavier Vadim!" he whispered to his family, then turned back to the phone and continued in his normal voice. "Xavier! Hello! How's Chicago?"

Xavier clearly wasn't in the mood for small talk.

"My daughter's friend is under the impression that your daughter has something that belongs to Veronique."

Roger swallowed hard, suddenly even more nervous than he had been a moment earlier. Why was this day going so wrong? Was Xavier Vadim really calling long distance to yell about a girl's diary?

"Well, yes," he stammered. "There was a girl, but it was actually pretty darned funny. We didn't understand her. A language barrier thing."

Xavier Vadim was unimpressed. "It is very important that Veronique gets her diary. You understand this, Roger, *oui*? You are a father. A daughter's secrets must be hers alone."

"I understand," Roger managed, though now he was even more convinced that the diary held some sort of clue. Though honest by nature, instinct told him to hide the truth. "If we find it, we'll be sure to let you know."

Even as he said the words, Roger saw Maddy clutching it.

Vadim's response was pure ice. "I have a better idea. You will leave the diary in an envelope with Camille's name just outside the front door. By sunrise."

Xavier clicked off. Roger's skin froze, but he forced a laugh. He couldn't alarm his family.

"I hear you, *mon ami*," he said to the dead line. "Make sure you get yourselves up the Sears Tower, OK? 'Bye now. *Au revoir*."

He hung up. "It's all good, Hitchcocks."

"Get real, Dad," Maddy said. "He had already hung up, right?"

"Well . . . sort of."

"OK," Benji said. "This is officially disturbing."

"What does he want?" Rebecca asked.

Roger tried to keep it light. "Well, we have to leave the diary in an envelope with Camille's name on it by sunrise. No biggie."

Rebecca was stunned. "So you told him we have it?"

"You heard me," Roger said. "I denied it completely— but he just knew, OK?"

"Make that officially highly disturbing," Benji said.

"It is," Maddy said. In the half-light she suddenly looked more like a little girl than the young woman she was in such a hurry to become. "What are we going to do?"

"I'll tell you what we're going to do" Rebecca said. "Call Harry Huberman!"

Roger couldn't have imagined a worse suggestion. Just what he needed—a suave embassy guy to use a simple case of mistaken identity to horn in on his wife.

"You can't call him," he said. "It's midnight."

Rebecca was already rummaging through her purse, looking for the number.

"Honey!" Roger went on. "That really isn't . . . "

He didn't finish the thought. How could he have been so stupid? It was there in front of him all the time.

"What is it, Daddy?" Maddy asked.

Roger pointed to the small wooden cabinet hanging in the front hallway. It was secured by a padlock.

"There it is," he whispered. "Vadim's *cachette*."

"Oh my God!" Maddy said. "It has to be."

"Nice, Dad," Benji said.

"See?" he said, turning to his wife. "We don't need help. We'll just look in Vadim's hiding place and figure this thing out all by ourselves."

Rebecca shook her head. "We are not breaking into a locked cabinet, OK? What if they broke into ours?"

But Roger had already caught a glimpse of the knife rack out of the corner of his eye.

"That's the beauty of it, sweets," Roger said, reaching for the smallest knife he could find. "They're not even going to know we peeked."

Roger lifted the cabinet off the wall and began to loosen the screws on its back. From her alarmed look, he could tell that the old nervous Rebecca was back in full force. For a moment he considered stopping. After all, he didn't want to jeopardize the gains he had made with his wife that afternoon and evening. But when the first screw came loose in his fingers, he dropped it on the kitchen counter and moved right on to the next. Yes, an otherwise fine day had taken a sharp turn into the world of scary and strange. But now that he was taking action, he couldn't stop.

"I can't believe it," Rebecca said. "Do you realize the lessons you're teaching these children?"

Maddy smiled. "They're not lessons if we already know them, Mom."

Rebecca let that one pass.

"What do you expect to find in there?"

Roger was lost in his own world—a world where he was no longer a mild-mannered commodities trader who had fallen on hard times as the result of a year of lice-infested corn. Instead, he was a dashing spy admired worldwide for his daring and style. The type of guy who relaxed by winning downhills using only a single ski and pole just to make it easy on the competition.

"*La fiole!*" he cried. "Second screw out!"

Benji clapped. "Two down, two to go! You go, Daddy-o!"

"We should not be taking apart the furniture,"

Rebecca scolded. She had begun to pace, red-faced. "We should be calling Harry Huberman. Maybe even the police. This is serious! Do you realize that a man approached you in the theater and asked you to get on a plane to Algiers? And that Benji pushed him down the stairs and we ran like criminals out of the opera? Now Xavier Vadim calls us making threats—and all about a girl's diary! No, no, no! Put that knife down, Roger. Now! We need help!"

"Got it!" Roger said.

All four screws were on the counter. Roger carefully removed the backside of the cabinet. As her kids pushed close, Rebecca sighed. She didn't approve of her husband's reckless behavior but still found herself strangely unable to suppress a small smile. Here was a side of Roger that she had never seen before. A braver side, a man who was willing to take risks.

"What's there?" she said.

Roger smiled at Rebecca. "It looks like you weren't the only one who hid the family pictures."

He reached into the back of the cabinet, pulled out a sheaf of photographs of the Vadims, and began to sort through them. But at first glance at the family with whom they had traded lives, Roger stopped short, breath held, too confused to speak.

"What's wrong, Dad?" Benji asked. "You look sick."

"Yeah," Maddy said. "Is it your turn to puke?"

Roger swallowed hard.

"Daddy?" Maddy said, more concerned now. "What is it?"

"These pictures," Roger stammered.

"What?" Rebecca said.

Roger held up a family portrait of a husband and wife and their daughter and son, then watched his own family's faces turn from wonder to surprise to fear.

"I don't get it," Rebecca said, voice shaking.

"Me neither," Maddy said.

"Those aren't the people staying in our house in Chicago," Benji said.

Indeed they weren't. The father was blond, the mother and daughter both redheads. The boy was three. Quickly, Roger rifled through the rest of the pictures. Every single one was of the same four people.

"Who are these people?" Maddy asked, grabbing the first family portrait. "The *real* Vadims?"

Roger suddenly wished with an overpowering desire that he had never gotten the idea to come to Paris.

"Hitchcocks," he said. "We're in trouble."

CHAPTER ELEVEN

"We. Are. Calling. Harry!"

Roger had rarely seen his wife look so determined. Rebecca fumbled for the phone and dialed. To her relief, Huberman answered on the second ring. He didn't sound like he had been asleep either.

"Mr. Huberman?" Rebecca began. "It's Rebecca Hitchcock. Yes, from the Eiffel Tower." She paused. "You've been thinking of me? How sweet."

Roger grabbed away the phone as Maddy rolled her eyes at Benji.

"Mr. Huberman?" Roger said, pacing the Vadim

kitchen. "Here's the situation. We did a house swap with a very nice family. At least we thought they were, but then we made the mistake of using their tickets to the opera, where I was approached by a strange Algerian man who wanted some MGF."

For the first time, Huberman spoke. "MGF?"

"Yes, yes!" Roger said. "Do you know what that means?"

"It means you need to meet me at the embassy."

Roger shuddered. "Really?"

"What's he saying?" Rebecca asked.

Roger cupped the mouthpiece and whispered to his family. "He says we need to meet him at the embassy."

"Thank God!" Rebecca said.

"It's across the Seine," Huberman went on.

Just then there was a small but distinct click on the line.

"What was that?' Huberman asked.

"I don't know," Roger said. "I heard it, too."

"What phone are you calling from?"

"The house line."

Huberman's voice remained calm. "Someone has been listening, Roger. Your lives could be in danger. Get out of there. Now! I will be waiting."

With that, the line went dead. Roger turned to his

family, trying to keep the panic from showing on his face.

"What's wrong?" Maddy said.

"Hitchcocks! To the embassy—on the double."

"Yes," Rebecca said. "Harry'll know what to do."

Maddy smiled. "Now you're on a first-name basis, Mom?"

Rebecca shot her daughter a hard glance. "I'm just saying that Harry knows Paris. He'll keep us safe."

"If we get to him in one piece, you mean." It was Benji calling from the window. "Look!"

Roger, Rebecca, and Maddy exchanged a terrified glance, then squeezed next to Benji. Down below, the tall man in the yellow suit—the Algerian—was entering the building.

"Oh my God," Rebecca whispered.

"This isn't good," Maddy said.

Benji was too terrified to say anything further.

"Hitchcocks," Roger said. "It's time to move!"

In the next moments the family gathered their things with a manic energy that might have seemed comic if they hadn't been so frightened. Rebecca grabbed Beatrix Vadim's stack of mad money. Maddy stuffed Veronique's diary in her back pants pocket while Roger tried to corral them all toward the door.

"Hurry!" Roger called. "He's coming!"

"I can't find our passports!" Benji cried.

"Forget them!" Roger said, and yanked his son toward the door.

"But Dad, what if . . . !"

"Later!" Roger said.

Benji allowed himself to be pushed into the hallway after his mother and sister.

"We'll go upstairs!" Roger called, following them out. "To the roof!"

But the Algerian was already only a floor away, seeming to all but glide toward them, moving effortlessly up the stairs, three at a time.

"Daddy!" Maddy cried.

"Oh my God!" Rebecca said.

"Change of plans!"

"This way, Dad!" Benji said. He pointed down a dark hall.

Which is when something extraordinary happened.

The Elevator Man leaped out of the shadows!

"Ah," he whispered. "*La famille Hitchcock.*"

As he spoke, Benji saw, lit by a lone lightbulb, two more scars to go with his pierced eyebrow.

By this point, any residue of calm on the part of the family had vanished. The Hitchcocks screamed as one.

"Daddy!" Benji cried. "Do something!"

His father lurched toward the door to the apartment, dragging the family along with him. But they weren't fast enough. With the Elevator Man hot on their heels, Rebecca and Maddy pressed their backs to the wall. As Benji dove on the ground, he saw his father turn to meet their assailant face-to-face.

"Leave us alone!" Roger cried.

For a split second, Benji felt a surge of hope. If his father could be that recklessly brave, anything seemed possible.

"You go, Dad!" Benji shouted.

"It's not *you* I want, Roger Hitchcock!" the Elevator Man shouted.

Benji gasped. With a quick stutter step, the Elevator Man cut around his father, leaped in the air . . . and tackled the Algerian.

"What?" Benji cried.

Working fast, Roger unlocked the door. "Inside!" he yelled.

Benji thought he was home free. His father, sister, and mother were already safe inside. The door was three short steps away. But then the Algerian flipped the Elevator Man down a flight of stairs and cut Benji off.

"Did you really think you could get away with

pushing me down the *opéra* stairs?"

Benji had a sudden vision: Wouldn't it be great to take the Algerian out with his Lego Death Star? But with no weapons real or imagined on hand, Benji was forced to rely on his wits. Seeing an opening, he dove under the Algerian's legs, then rolled sideways into the apartment foyer.

"Ah!" the Algerian said. "Stop!"

Roger slammed the door hard and flipped the bolt. The Algerian pounded with both fists.

"Nice move, Benj!" Maddy said, helping him to his feet.

"That ought to hold him," Roger said.

"What now?" Rebecca asked.

"I saw a terrace," Maddy said. "We can jump off of it to the adjacent roof."

"Works for me," Benji said.

"Jump off a terrace?" Rebecca said. "The hell we are!"

"The other roof isn't far," Maddy said. "Three feet tops."

Thwap! Thwap! Thwap!

"Doesn't look like we have a choice," Roger said. "Come on!"

He led his family down the back hallway to the

master bedroom. As Maddy had noticed, a small door led to a narrow terrace.

"Our escape route," Roger said.

Thwap! Thwap!

"What's that Algerian using now?" Maddy asked. "A sledgehammer?"

"Maybe an ax!" Benji said.

Another boom shook the walls.

"How about a battering ram?" Maddy said.

"Everyone outside," Roger said.

Soon the family was scrunched together on the small terrace. The streets of Paris stretched out below them, lovely and inviting. Though it was late, there were people on the street, still enjoying everything the city had to offer. But now wasn't the time to take in the sights. It was the time to run for their lives. As Maddy had noticed, an adjacent roof stood about three feet away.

"Well," Roger said to Rebecca with a half smile. "I said Paris would be an adventure, right?"

Without another word, he leaped from the terrace onto the roof of the adjacent building. Though the jump was a bit longer than he had anticipated, he was sure not to let his family notice.

"Come on," he said. "Benji next. Straight into my

arms. I'll catch you!"

Now Benji swallowed hard. Sports were never his forte. Standing on the tiny terrace, he thought back to gym class. When tested for general athletic ability, only two other people in his grade had scored lower. Worse, he had come in last in the long jump. What were the odds he could make it across a three-foot chasm to an opposite building with an insane Algerian out for blood?

"I'm a thinker, not a doer!" Benji cried.

"Not true," Maddy said. "A minute ago you scrambled under the Algerian's legs."

"I wasn't thinking. I just acted."

"Act again," his sister said. "Take my hand. And don't look down."

"Maddy," Rebecca said. "I don't like this."

Thwap! Thwap! Thwap!

"You got a better idea?" Maddy asked. She turned to her brother. "OK, ready? One, two . . . three!"

An excellent leaper, Maddy all but pulled her brother off the terrace onto the other roof. Benji landed awkwardly on his knees.

"Nice, sport!" Roger said.

Benji nodded. Maybe next year he'd hire a mad killer to chase him when he did the phys ed long jump.

He turned to his mother.

"Your turn!"

Rebecca made the mistake of glancing down—all six floors. Suddenly dizzy, she felt like she was going to pitch forward.

"Come on, Mom!" Maddy called.

"I can't!" she said.

"If I did it, you can, too," Benji said.

"Stop looking down," Roger said. "Just jump."

"We'll catch you!" Maddy said.

Then the family heard it: the loudest *thwap* of them all, followed by the sound of ripping wood. Rebecca wheeled around, trembling.

"What was that?" she asked.

"He's splintered the door," Roger said.

Rebecca needed no more encouragement. Before anyone in her family could say another word, she flung herself into the air, arms and legs akimbo, then fell hard on the opposite roof. As Roger helped her to her feet, they heard the footsteps.

"He's inside!" Benji said. "Haul it."

"This way!" Roger said.

Scrambling across the rooftop, Benji was dimly aware that it was a lovely night—the perfect evening to be in Paris—if only he wasn't running faster than he had ever had to run in his life. At Camp Keys his biggest fear would have been performing a sonata at the talent show. Or maybe making sure not to get water up his nose in the shallow end of the pool. But now wasn't the time to ruminate over what could have been. Running as hard as he could, he followed his dad around a chimney, splashed through a puddle of old rainwater, then circled around a water tower.

Then there it was—a thin line in the darkness: the opposite edge.

Benji gasped. "Oh, no! No way!"

This time, the next building over was a good four feet away.

"We can make it," Maddy called. "It's not far."

"For you, maybe," Benji said.

His sister wasn't slowing down for anything. When Rebecca shouted, "Maddy, don't!" she was already in the air, landing easily on the adjacent building.

"Relax, Mom," Maddy said, looking back. "Gymnastics, remember? Come on, Benji! You next!"

Benji made the same mistake his mother had made on the terrace: He looked down, six floors to an alley of garbage cans.

"Oh, cripes!" he said.

"Pretend there's a dog at your heels!"

Benji gasped. A dog! Some days it seemed like every family in their neighborhood but them had a giant, vicious dog. Avoiding the yapping beasts on the short walk to school was a daily trial.

"Benji!" his mother said. "Don't!"

"Relax, Mom! I'm on it!"

Benji visualized a particularly large and excitable German shepherd that lived around the corner—a dog who had taken a piece out of his shirt more than once—and ran for the edge. Throwing himself into the air, he gathered just enough momentum to make it to the lip of the opposite building.

"See?" Maddy said, hauling him in. "Easy!"

A new sound followed them now—one more terrifying than a dog. The heavy footsteps of a human being.

"Oh my God," Rebecca said. She glanced over her shoulder. "It's him!"

Roger grabbed his wife's hand. Together they jumped across, stumbling onto the adjacent roof.

"Get up!" Benji called as they landed. "He's coming!"

The Algerian was moving so quickly he looked like a blur of yellow. Escape seemed impossible. But once again, the Hitchcocks got a helping hand: The Elevator Man leaped out of the darkness, this time landing on the Algerian's back.

"Yes!" Maddy said. "Run!"

But Benji couldn't resist. Ten feet along the other roof, he turned. To his dismay, a few short seconds was all it had taken for the Algerian to put the Elevator Man in a headlock. Then he pushed the Elevator Man off the edge. Benji screamed—but then, a miracle. The Elevator Man managed to grab hold of a balcony railing two floors down and swing himself onto the lower terrace.

"No way that elevator guy isn't some sort of major-league spy," Maddy said, coming to her brother's side.

Benji nodded. "Normal people just don't do stuff like that."

"Come on!" Roger said. "We aren't safe yet."

From across the divide between the two buildings, the Algerian's voice pierced the night sky.

"No use running, Monsieur Vadim. You'll never get away."

Roger thought he had been frightened a year earlier when he had set their tent on fire at Yosemite, but this was a fear of an altogether different nature—a sharp terror mixed with confusion. Why couldn't this Algerian get the point?

"I'm not Vadim!" he cried desperately. "I know corn, not the MGF!"

"You are lying!"

The Algerian leaped across the chasm onto the second building.

"Run!" Roger called to his family. "Run!"

Benji didn't need to be told twice. Scurrying madly ahead, he muttered wildly to himself, "I'm dead. So dead. Seriously dead. Mozart dead. Isaac Newton dead."

As for Rebecca, she was almost too scared to run. Maybe the Algerian would listen to logic? If they could just go back to the apartment and find their passports, they could prove that they weren't the Vadims, right? She gave it one last try.

"We are not the Vadims!" she shouted.

Then she gasped. What was that glinting in the Algerian's hand?

"It's a gun!" Roger said.

The Algerian laughed. Roger and Rebecca were running across the roof, expecting to feel bullets rip into their bodies at any second, when they suddenly ran smack into Maddy. Rebecca fell to her knees. Roger blinked. His daughter had stopped on a skylight and was pointing down to a teenage boy—who was standing by an easel, holding a paintbrush.

"Look!" she said. "It's that kid, Stephan! From Veronique's diary!"

"Cool," Benji said, doubling back. "But can we chat about it later?"

With a startling crack, the glass beneath them shattered. The family fell en masse ten feet down directly onto the boy's bed.

"*Bonjour*," Maddy said as the Hitchcocks untangled themselves. "You must be Stephan."

The boy looked as though he had just been visited by a family of spirits.

"Sweetie," Rebecca said. "This is no time for introductions, OK? We're being hunted down by a crazed Algerian."

"Sorry to drop in like this," Roger said. "But we're outta here."

Up above, the family could hear rapidly approaching footsteps.

"This way," Benji said, heading to the door.

Again, Maddy hesitated. Her eye had caught the boy's painting. It was of a pretty girl with a shallow cleft on her chin and long red hair.

"Is that Veronique?" Maddy asked.

Too shocked to talk, Stephan managed a nod.

"Good news," Maddy said. "She's way into you."

Stephan blinked. "Way into me? You know this?"

"I read her diary!"

Maddy felt her father yank her by the arm to the door.

"You're really an amazing artist," she said before sprinting after her family down the stairs. From a floor below, she heard the Algerian jump from the roof to Stephan's floor. But their assailant didn't stop to admire the boy's work.

"*Arrêtez, Monsieur Vadim!*" he called from the boy's door. "You're just making it harder on yourself!"

By that time, Rebecca was leading the family down a narrow circular staircase.

"Hurry, Mom!" Benji cried.

"I'm going as fast as I can!"

"Go faster!" Roger said.

"Monsieur Vadim!" came the voice from above.

"I'm not Vadim!" Roger shouted.

"Do not lie to me!"

"Step on it!" Maddy called.

Rebecca missed the next step completely, tripped, and tumbled down the flight of stairs.

"Mom!" Benji called. "Are you okay?"

"Fine," Rebecca stammered. She tried to stand and instantly fell back over. "I think I sprained my ankle."

Roger raced down the stairs, hoisted his wife onto his back, fireman style—this time not for laughs—and continued down the stairs.

"Hey, nice, Dad!" Benji said.

"Come on!" Roger called. "Only one more flight!"

But Benji and Maddy knew that their father could only hold on for so long. By the time the Hitchcocks reached the street, the Algerian was right behind and Roger was sucking wind.

"Run!" Benji cried.

"Dad!" Maddy said.

But it was no use. Benji knew that any second now the Algerian would jump on their father's back. Then it would all be over. But Benji hadn't counted on the tenacity of the Elevator Man. Appearing from out of nowhere, the strange and persistent man with the pierced eyebrow jumped from a second-floor balcony and landed right on the Algerian's back.

"Run!" Benji said.

Moments later the children were following their father into traffic on Boulevard St.-Germain. A taxi driver slammed on the brakes. A headlight shone right in Maddy's eyes.

"Do you even know where the embassy is?" Rebecca called.

"Across the Seine," Roger said. "Come on! Every-one in the cab!"

After a short ride through the Paris night, the cab stopped in front of an elegant four-story building of white stone.

"*L'ambassade américaine,*" the driver said.

Roger looked out the window. The American flag waved above the main entrance. No Fourth of July parade or rendition of "The Star-Spangled Banner" had ever made him feel more patriotic.

"Yes!" he shouted.

"Oh my gosh!" Maddy gasped. "That is a sight!"

"Chicago, here we come!" Benji said.

Rebecca threw a handful of Euros at the driver, and the family poured out of the cab.

"Look!" Rebecca said. "It's Harry!"

He was standing beside a black limo that was parked in front of the embassy. Even in the middle of the night, he looked immaculate in a suit and tie.

"Get inside," Huberman said. "Quickly!"

A day earlier, Roger would have been jealous. Now he was thrilled. How fortunate to have met this helpful man at the Eiffel Tower. Who cared if he had an unspeakably beautiful chin? Seconds later, the family was safely in the back of a plush limousine. The driver was a heavyset Asian man with a bowl haircut. Huberman jumped in next to Roger.

"The Algerian is chasing us," Roger said. "He thinks I'm Vadim! We also found a diary. Show him, Maddy."

Maddy handed it to Huberman. "It says that Vadim stole some sort of a vial."

"It's okay," Harry Huberman said reassuringly. He tucked the diary into his jacket pocket. "You've done well. You're safe now."

Maddy leaned back in her seat. Now that she was safe, she realized how scared she had been. Her heart was more lurching in her chest than pounding. As she tried to gain control of her breathing, Huberman leaned toward the driver and said something in rapid Chinese. Why would an American Embassy official have a Chinese driver? How many languages did Huberman speak, anyway? Maddy was about to ask when a fist hit the window. Standing outside was the Algerian—again!

"Let's move it, shall we?" Huberman said.

The driver peeled away from the curb. Maddy looked out the rearview mirror just in time to see the Elevator Man rise once again out of nowhere to throw the Algerian to the pavement. This time he made it stick. After a short struggle, the tenacious man in the yellow suit was in handcuffs.

"The Elevator Man had to be a cop," Benji said. "Cool."

"Yeah," Maddy said. "Whoever he is, thank God he's on our side."

As she turned around to face forward, she caught her breath. Strangely, Harry Huberman was putting on a gas mask.

"Say there, Huberman?" her father was asking. "What are you doing?"

Maddy noticed that the driver had on a gas mask, too. Something wasn't right. Though the mask covered most of his face, Maddy could see Harry Huberman allow himself a small grin. He looked directly at her father.

"You called the wrong man, Mr. Hitchcock."

A light orange mist began to fill the back of the car. It smelled sickly sweet, almost as if someone were cooking an extra-rich dessert and had doubled the sugar.

"What's going on?" Maddy said.

She reached for the door handle. Before her hand was halfway there, she slumped against the window, out cold.

CHAPTER TWELVE

As the limo carrying the family Hitchcock sped into the dark night, their one true friend walked into Interpol Headquarters in Lyon, France. Instead of wearing the ragged clothes of the Elevator Man, Jules Camus—for that was his real name— was dressed in a well-pressed shirt and slacks. Around his waist was a holster that held a standard-issue revolver, the type of gun preferred by French Interpol agents.

Slowly, he made his way up the stairs to the second floor. Down a long corridor, he stopped at an office with a glass window that read COMMISSIONER BERNARD FROMIQUE.

With a sigh, the Elevator Man paused for a moment. It didn't matter that he was one of the best agents in the service or that he had finally captured the irritating Algerian. He had let the Hitchcocks get away. Worse, he still hadn't tracked down the exact location of the MGF. Commissioner Fromique was known to remove agents from cases for less.

"This could get ugly," Jules warned himself.

Still, there was nothing to be gained from more delay. With a deep breath, he rapped twice on the door. A voice from inside answered immediately.

"Yes, come!"

Jules pushed open the door. The commissioner was looking out the window, back turned. Jules could only imagine the unsatisfied scowl on his face. The famous jowls would be drooping even more than usual.

"You wanted to see me, sir?"

The commissioner turned around. Indeed, he was frowning heavily. Of course, Commissioner Fromique rarely looked happy. But today he looked downright miserable.

"It was such a simple task, Jules."

The Elevator Man knew what was required of him:

Make no effort to defend himself. Simply nod and take the blame.

"I understand, sir."

"Watch the Hitchcocks. That's all I wanted." Fromique rubbed a hand through his thick, graying hair. "I hate failure, Jules."

The Elevator Man nodded gravely. He knew he deserved it, but that didn't make it any more pleasant. And the commissioner had a way of drawing things out, almost taking twisted enjoyment in reprimanding an agent.

"Not more than me, I promise you," Jules said.

With that, Fromique took another long look out the window, as if contemplating whether to throw Jules out of it. Finally, the commissioner turned back around.

"All right, sit," he said.

Jules did as he was told. The commissioner took his own seat and leaned back in the chair.

"In any case," he went on, "the Hitchcocks aren't our first concern, are they? Our first concern is . . . "

The commissioner's voice rose at the end of the thought, telling Jules that he was expected to fill in the blank.

"To find the MGF, sir."

The commissioner's eyes narrowed. From up close,

his jowls seemed to droop almost all the way down to his shoulders. For a moment, Jules imagined that he was chatting with a giant St. Bernard.

"Don't finish my sentences, Jules."

"Of course not, sir."

"Just show me what you have."

Jules was ready. He pulled a folder out of his briefcase and revealed a collection of photos. The first was of the Hitchcocks at the Eiffel Tower. The second was of a small blue vial.

"One hundred milliliters of MGF went missing from a secured lab at La Polytechnique Française on June twenty-third."

The commissioner rubbed his chin. "And this Algerian? He was chasing the MGF?"

The Elevator Man flipped to the third picture, a mug shot of the Algerian.

"His name is Aljan Aljani and he isn't talking. We believe that he's employed by Hazan Oil, the largest petroleum concern in Dubai, and that he was attempting to secure the MGF from Xavier Vadim on their behalf."

The commissioner moved his right hand over his shoulder in a futile attempt to scratch an impossible-to-reach itch on the small of his back.

"What is this MGF?" he said, thinking out loud. "Venezuela, the Chinese, the Arab republics. Everybody's chasing it." He finally gave up on getting the itch with his hand and rubbed his back against the seat. "Do we believe the vial may be in Chicago?"

Jules nodded. "I am liaising with the FBI as we speak."

The commissioner allowed himself a small smile, the first since Jules had entered.

"But you are not liaising with the FBI as we speak. You are liaising with *me* as we speak."

The Elevator Man swallowed hard. "That is correct, sir. I misspoke."

The commissioner leaned forward in the chair. His face was grave. "Just find that vial."

Jules exhaled, greatly relieved. He had worried that the commissioner was going to pull him from the case.

"Thank you, sir. I will, sir."

"Good. Now, how about the Hitchcocks?"

"What about them, sir?"

"They don't have the MGF, do they?"

Jules paused. The Hitchcocks seemed too naive to be involved in an international conspiracy. Then again, anything was possible.

"That's what we're trying to figure out."

The commissioner stroked his chin. "And where are they now?"

Jules hated to admit it, but he never believed in lying, not even to cover for himself.

"To tell the truth, I have no idea."

CHAPTER THIRTEEN

Benji was the first Hitchcock to stir, waking from a dreamless slumber, his face planted firmly on a hard, wood floor. He rubbed his eyes, then groaned, a sharp pain shooting through the back of his neck. Then he rolled over, blinked at a strange, barren ceiling, then finally sat up and looked at his family sprawled around him. His mother was on her back, arms splayed out from her sides, mouth open. Maddy's body was curled in a giant C, her head on her mother's stomach. His father was lying on his stomach across the room by a fireplace.

Benji inhaled sharply. Was he the only survivor? Had he been left in a room with his dead family? How had they gotten here? Terrified, he scrambled from his mother to his sister to his father to make sure they were breathing. Satisfied, he finally exhaled. Then he rose shakily to his feet and tried the door. Just as he thought—locked.

There was a slim shaft of light from the lone window. Time to see where they were. Pulling aside the frayed curtain, Benji couldn't tell much—only that he and his family were trapped on the second floor of a small house. Outside was a beat-up green tractor and a rusty Honda. Beyond that were miles of ragged cornfields. A thin dirt road wended its way toward a nearby mountain.

"Great," he thought. "Kidnapped in the middle of nowhere."

It was all too much. A boy like him didn't belong in some sort of weird European plot. He belonged at Camp Keys, practicing piano and reconfiguring hard drives. Staring out the window, he imagined performing the Chopin *Revolutionary* Etude for a captive audience, then sneaking out of his cabin at night to name constellations. But this was no time to be lost in useless fantasies. This was one of those defining life moments when heroes in books and movies found unknown reserves of courage. Benji sighed. He was no movie star, just a nerdy kid. For a moment he fought to keep his composure. Then he gave in and let the tears come.

"Hey, wingman?"

Benji kept on sniffling.

"Wingman?" He felt his father's hand on his shoulder. "You OK?"

The boy turned slowly. A moment ago he would have been thrilled to see another family member awake. Now he was embarrassed. Whatever had been in that gas was obviously wearing off. The entire family was coming to.

"I'm fine, Dad."

"You don't look fine," Maddy said groggily from the floor. "You're crying."

"Was not," Benji said.

Maddy saw him wipe his face with his sleeve but kept her mouth shut. Of course he was crying. She felt like crying, too. Who wouldn't? The last thing she remembered was the sickly sweet smell of the orange gas. Being abducted seemed a lot more romantic in the movies. In real life it was, well, terrifying. Then Maddy felt her mother stir beneath her. Rebecca took a good look at their new surroundings, then glanced pointedly at Roger.

"I take it we aren't in Paris anymore," she said.

Maddy saw her father's face cloud over.

"I guess not," he said. "And I guess that calling Harry Huberman wasn't such a great idea."

It was a low blow, but Maddy didn't blame her dad for saying it. Her mother had seemed pretty enamored of the guy—and why, really? Had they trusted their lives to Harry Huberman because he wore a nice suit and had a great cleft?

Maddy's mom didn't seem to think so. She stood up so fast, Maddy's head fell from her stomach to the hard floor.

"Excuse me?" she said to her husband. "You're blaming this on me?"

"Well," Roger said. "You're the one who wanted to call your *friend* from the embassy."

"You're the one who wanted to do this stupid house swap in the first place." Rebecca wheeled around, taking in the barren room. "Look where we are. Nice trip to *Paris*, Roger!"

Maddy grimaced. At least Benji had the courage to admit he was frightened. But her parents? It was painful to see two adults taking their terror out on each other.

"Just relax, OK?" Roger said. "I'm going to get us out of here."

Maddy rose to her feet.

"How? We're probably surrounded by a moat or something."

"Actually, just lots of corn," Benji said.

"Well, I'm not standing for it," Rebecca said. "Time to get out of here."

Maddy knew that tone of voice. When her mother was fed up, she could morph into something truly scary, capable of getting pretty much whatever she wanted. She watched her mother stride purposefully across the room—all traces of the sprained ankle were gone—and shake the doorknob with two fists.

"Let us out! We're American citizens! That's the United States! You wanna have the CIA breathing down your throats?"

"Sorry, Mom," Maddy said. "Getting out of here may not be quite as easy as talking your way onto a direct flight to Paris from Miami."

Rebecca shot her daughter a "don't mess with me" look, then faced Roger. "You know what? Next time you want to go on one of these stupid family vacations, go yourself!"

"Nice, Mom," Maddy said. "That's real helpful."

"Watch your tone, young lady."

"Come on, sweetie," Roger said. "Maddy's right. That's not helping, is it?"

Maddy knew that being helpful was no longer an option. When her mother didn't get something she had screamed for, what generally followed was a total breakdown.

"Not helping? I'll tell you what isn't helping! I'm sick of being hauled around the world like a sack of . . . of volleyballs!"

Maddy saw her father blink. Her mother had hit below the belt: She had impugned the tradition of the family vacation.

"Oh yeah?" her father said. "Well, I'm sick of you acting like a volleyball all the time."

Maddy shot her brother a glance. Benji looked stunned, as though he were watching Charles Darwin speak out against his theory of evolution.

"What?" Rebecca said. "Are you calling me a volley-ball?"

Roger didn't back down. "Yes, as a matter of fact, I am! You, my dear, are a volleyball!"

If her father's words weren't laced with such anger and fear, they would have been comical. As for Maddy, she was stunned, too, for once stripped bare of any sort of tart rejoinder or comment. But just like that, the argument was cut off at the knees. A deathly wail filled the room. Maddy had heard it before, the last time when Benji's Lego Death Star had been blown onto the floor by a windstorm.

"Shut up!" her brother cried. "Shut up!" He turned to their mother. "Stop being mean to Daddy!"

This time the tears came so hard there was no stopping them. Maddy saw her parents exchange a guilty glance. Rebecca went instantly to Benji.

"I'm not being mean to Daddy," she said, wrapping an arm around him. She looked desperately at Roger, then back at Benji. "Uh, we're discussing, dear. This is how grown-ups discuss."

Rebecca's explanation only served to make Benji cry even harder. He pushed his mother away.

"Well, stop discussing!" he slobbered. "I'm scared!"

"Hey, we're all scared," Maddy said. "But we have to keep it together, right?"

"Oh, thanks," Benji said. "Who told you that? Noah Willis?"

Now it was Maddy's turn to be shocked.

"Hey, shut up."

"You shut up! I'm really, *really* scared!"

Maddy grimaced. Just what they needed now.

Another fear-induced argument. No doubt about it: Her brother was good for solving equations but lousy in a crisis.

"Come on," she said. "Pull it together, OK?"

Benji sank to his knees.

"I want to go home!"

"We will, honey," Rebecca said. "Just as soon as we get out of here."

"You'll be tickling Chopin on the old ivories before you know it, sport."

Benji jumped up and down like a three-year-old having a tantrum.

"No! I want to go home now!"

Maddy had heard enough. If ever a situation called for an intervention, this was it. Though she and Benji had been on bad terms for the school year, she had never hit him. But now it was her turn to act on her fears. Before she knew what she was doing, she cocked her arm and slapped him hard on the cheek. For a spilt second, the family was silent, trying to take in what had just happened.

"Ow!" Benji said finally, eyes wide. "You . . . you *hit* me!"

Maddy felt terrible.

"Oh, God, Benji."

Before she could finish, he flung himself at her, grabbed her around the waist, and tackled her hard against the floor. Maddy was so surprised it took her a few moments to fight back. Her brother was a wimp—a giant brain coated in a thin layer of pale skin and glasses. She doubted that he even knew how to make a fist. Still, he had done it. And now she had to take matters in hand.

"OK, I hit you!" Maddy cried. "Because you needed it."

She flipped him onto his back easily and pinned him to the floor.

"Stop fighting!" Rebecca called. "Both of you!"

Benji landed a punch in Maddy's gut. It hurt more than she ever would have expected.

"You'll pay for that!"

"Break it up!" Roger said.

By that point, Maddy had Benji in a half nelson. Maddy felt her father lift her up and shake Benji loose. Then he deposited her on the floor on the other side of the room.

"You know our family rules," Rebecca said. "No fighting!"

"We weren't fighting," Benji said. His shirt was untucked and his eyes were red. His hair stuck out in too many directions to count.

"Yeah, Mom," Maddy said with a wry grin. "We were *discussing!*"

Her mother's eyes went wide. It took Maddy a moment to realize that she was looking beyond her toward the door. Framed in the doorway stood a squat older woman. Turning to face her, Maddy thought she had never seen a human being who was so wide and wrinkled.

"Madame!" Roger said. "We are the Hitchcocks of Chicago. And we demand to know where we are." He forced himself to take another step closer. *"Comprendez-vous?"*

"We have rights guaranteed by the Geneva Convention!" Rebecca said. She looked at her husband. "Maybe she's Sofia." She turned back to the woman. "Are you Sofia?"

It was then that Maddy noticed the tray. On it were four bowls filled with a grayish substance she assumed was some sort of food. With a dismissive grunt in a language Maddy didn't understand—it certainly wasn't English or French—the woman laid the tray on the floor.

As the woman turned for the door, Maddy exchanged a glance with her parents. Somehow, she knew that their only hope for escape lay in delaying her. Clearly, Benji was thinking the same thing.

"Wait!" Benji cried. All eyes turned his way. He paused. What should he say?

The woman replied in a voice that sounded like a bark.

Maddy held her breath.

"I—I gotta pee!"

The woman frowned. "Pee?" she said in twisted English.

"Yes! Yes!" Maddy said. "He has to go. You know, go pee. Urinate."

"It's a basic human right!" Roger declared.

"Where do you expect us to do it?" Rebecca said. She glanced over her shoulder at the fireplace. "In there?"

The woman looked at the fireplace as if considering whether or not it could, in fact, be used as a bathroom. Finally, she scowled at Benji and nodded, then waved him to the door.

"Me?" Benji squeaked.

"He can't go alone," Rebecca said. "I'll go with him."

When his mother grabbed the door, the woman pushed her hard to the floor.

"No," the woman said.

Maddy saw the woman grab her brother by the collar and shove him out of the room. The door slammed shut.

CHAPTER FOURTEEN

Benji Hitchcock was many things. He was smart, that was for certain. He knew a lot about gadgets and computers. He had an unstoppable memory and played a mean piano. His report cards were filled with phrases such as "sweetly intelligent," "remarkably insightful," and "a joy to teach." But like many intelligent boys, there were other ways he would have preferred to have been described. "Courageous," for one. Or "daring." Maybe even "studly and dangerous."

But maybe, just maybe, he was more studly and dangerous than he thought. Hadn't he pushed a man down a flight of stairs, then run for his life across a Parisian rooftop? Hadn't he been kidnapped? Most important of all, hadn't he just body slammed his sister? In truth, Maddy had quickly wrestled him to the ground, but with that one act, Benji had showed himself that he was quickly morphing from the little boy who slept at the foot of his parents' bed into a more confident young man who could rise to the occasion. Following the old lady down a dimly lit hallway to a steep stairway, he was determined to do whatever it took to free his family.

But how?

Since their arrival in Paris, bad luck had followed the Hitchcocks around like a hungry dog begging for scraps at a feast. As Benji stepped into a small kitchen–living room area, the family finally caught a break. The old woman gestured down the hall and grunted.

Quickly, Benji surveyed the scene. Leaning back in a ripped lounge chair with a shotgun in his lap sat an old man watching a soccer game on a black-and-white TV. Worse, there was the small matter of the dog—a German shepherd, Benji guessed—tied by a rope to a small chair, lying right in front of the kitchen counter, growling, and chomping furiously on a bone.

That was the bad luck. The good luck was what lay

on the kitchen counter. There, next to an upside-down coffeepot, lay a set of keys. And not just any keys. Even from a distance, Benji could tell that they were too long and narrow to be to a house.

He glanced out the window. In the driveway stood the old Honda. Did it have gas? Could they use it to escape?

Again the woman pointed down the hall.

Benji drew in a deep breath. The path to the facilities took him directly past the dog. To make clear who controlled the territory, the animal instantly flew to the end of his leash, barking wildly. Panicked, Benji pressed himself against the wall.

"Down, boy," Benji stammered.

The man looked over his shoulder and yelled at the dog. Then an old boot flew across the room, catching the dog in the snout. With a whimper, the animal slunk back to the counter.

With the path cleared, Benji all but ran down the hall and shut the bathroom door. For a second he considered staying inside forever. Or else breaking out the small window over the toilet and running for help. But where? No, the only way out was in the car. And for that he needed the keys. It had already occurred to him what he had to do to get them. But did he have the guts? Even the little Corgi who lived next door in Chicago terrified him—and this dog was much bigger and meaner than that.

Benji washed his hands twice, then stared himself down in the mirror. Yes, he was the most unlikely hero on the planet, every inch a standard-issue American geek. But what was the fury of a crazed dog compared with his family's well-being? And so Benji dug deep— no, he wasn't an action hero from the movies or a book, but that didn't mean he couldn't do what had to be done. To hesitate was to chicken out. . . .

Benji kicked open the bathroom door. Marching down the hall like an army commando on a raid, he reached the living room, then immediately pretended to slip, making sure to cuff the dog firmly on the chin. As expected, the animal exploded in a fury of barks and yelps. As the old man lumbered over from his chair, waving another shoe and screaming for quiet, Benji struggled to his feet, slipped his hand onto the counter, and took the car keys. The woman grabbed him by the back of the shirt.

As the man dragged the dog back to his place by the counter, the woman pulled Benji by the scruff of his neck up the stairs. She opened the door to the Hitchcocks' room and shoved him inside. Benji hadn't seen his mother look so distraught since he had placed second in the statewide math competition. Her face was bone white.

"Oh my God! We heard the dog. What happened? Are you all right?"

"You OK, sport?" his father asked.

"We thought he had ripped you to shreds," Maddy said.

By that time Benji was smiling.

"No such luck, Sis."

Then his smile turned into a full-out grin.

His mother eyed him warily. "What's so funny?"

Benji opened his right fist, revealing the car keys.

"Who wants to take a ride?"

Benji couldn't believe where he was. It was one thing to provoke a vicious dog in order to steal a set of car keys. It was quite another to find himself standing atop his sister's shoulders halfway up a chimney. Of course, Benji knew that he had no one to blame but himself. When he stole the keys, he had had no clue as to how he and his family might actually break out of the room and get to the driveway. *Someone will think of something*, he thought. That someone was his father.

Now he was covered in soot, reaching desperately for the roof.

"Push me higher!" Benji called down.

"Yeah," Maddy said. "Hurry!"

Benji's foot slipped off his sister's shoulders and accidentally whacked her in the mouth.

"Hey, watch it!"

"Sorry!" Benji said. "I'm trying to stand still."

"Try harder!"

"OK!" Benji heard his mother call up. "Hold on."

Benji steadied himself on his sister's shoulders and looked up to the thin patch of daylight ten or so feet overhead. At the sound of a loud scuffling below, he looked down. He couldn't see much but knew that his mom was ducking into the fireplace, just like he and Maddy had done. Now it was her turn to put Maddy on her shoulders, thereby lifting Benji closer to the roof.

"All right," Benji heard. "One, two, three!"

Benji didn't move. He heard a crash, then a short scream, followed by his father hissing. "Quiet. Try again." A series of grunts later, Benji braced himself for the second attempt.

"OK. One! Two! Three!"

Wham! Up he went. In fact, his mother had done so well that Benji wasn't even ready for it. He shot up five and a half more feet, but to the left, scraping his head against the brick chimney wall, scuffing his face, and turning his glasses crooked.

"Watch it!" he said. "I almost lost my glasses!"

"Want to switch places?" Rebecca called up. "My back is already toast."

"Oh, just shush up," Maddy said. "Benji, can you reach the roof?"

Benji looked up. The pale blue sky was brighter. But he was too far away to shinny up.

"Sorry, no," he called. "I can't reach. We need Dad."

"All right," he heard his father call from down below. "Hold on, Hitchcocks!"

Benji wasn't the only Hitchcock who was discovering newfound reservoirs of strength and courage on the vacation. To his surprise, he soon felt himself being lifted up even higher. Just like that, the cool morning air was on his face. He wobbled dangerously to his right, then managed to pull himself onto the roof. Then Maddy passed him an end of the curtain that his father had just ripped from the window. Quickly, Benji tied it around the top of the chimney.

"OK," he shouted down. "We're good!"

A few moments later, Maddy used the curtain to pull herself out. Now it was Rebecca's turn.

"Hurry, Mom!"

"I wasn't made for this!"

"Neither were any of us!" Roger said. "Just climb!"

Benji could make out the dim form of his mother moving slowly up the chimney, with his father below, pushing her up. Soon she was crawling out onto the roof, next to her daughter and son.

"OK, Dad," Benji called down. "You next."

Benji expected to hear his father's usual plucky voice echo up the chimney. Instead, there was a loud grunt, followed by a bump and an "oof!"

"Dad?"

"I'm fine," Roger said. "Just slipped. I'm coming up."

"Hurry!" Rebecca said.

Benji, Maddy, and Rebecca peered down the dark chimney. Below, a dim outline of a man was trying to find a foothold, only to slip again.

"This isn't good," Benji said.

Then things got worse. Atop the roof, Benji, Rebecca, and Maddy heard the door to the room below creak open, followed by footsteps and a terrifying *pop! pop! pop!*

"What's that?" Rebecca asked tensely.

"Oh no!" Benji said. "I saw a shotgun in the living room!"

Rebecca went white. "Has someone shot your father?"

For a split second, Benji, Maddy, and Rebecca were frozen, too terrified to speak or move. But then Roger's head suddenly popped out of the chimney.

"Dad!" Maddy said. "You're alive!"

Roger hauled himself onto the roof. "Nothing like a few gunshots to give a guy motivation to climb."

Another round of *pops!* pierced the air.

"Was it the old man?" Benji shouted.

Roger nodded. "Yep. And he didn't pause to say hello."

"Let's get to that car!" Maddy said.

It was easier said than done. The roof slanted sharply downward. With no time to edge down on their backsides, the family had to take their chances on their feet. But no more than a step or two from the chimney, a flurry of *pops!* ripped a hole in the old roof. Just like that, the Hitchcocks found themselves looking into the room where they had been held captive. The old man was looking up through the barrel of the shotgun.

Pop! Pop! Pop!

The Hitchcocks danced to the roof's edge.

"Down the drainpipe!" Maddy said.

One by one, they half slid, half fell to the ground,

then moved quickly across the yard to the car.

"Keys!" Rebecca called. "I need the keys!"

Benji tossed them to his mom. "Here!"

In a flash, Maddy was in the backseat and Rebecca behind the wheel. Before Roger and Benji could make it in, the front door of the house flew open and the old man emerged, gun at the ready. Almost worse was what galloped after him: the giant dog, snarling madly, dragging the chair by the chain.

"Yikes!" Benji said.

At that moment, every bit of bravery the boy had exhibited that afternoon in the face of the dreaded beast disappeared. As if seeking payback, the dog ran straight for Benji.

"In the car!" Roger cried. "In the car!"

Terrified, Benji jumped—but in the wrong direction. Then he ran. Tripping on a hedge, he sprawled flat on the ground. He rolled over to see the giant dog bounding toward him, teeth bared, tongue flapping, a lion going after a lame zebra. Benji didn't try to run. He didn't raise his fists to fight. Swallowed by terror, he closed his eyes, fully prepared to be mauled. But then the dog's wild barks changed to frustrated yips. Slowly, Benji opened his eyes and gasped. Yes! A reprieve! The chair had gotten caught on the beat-up tractor. The dog was frantically trying to get himself loose, pulling on the rope and sprawling backward.

"Run!" Roger called to his son. "Hurry!"

Benji didn't need to be told twice. Up on his feet, he sprinted for the car. As another round of buckshot filled the air, he dove into the backseat next to his sister. By that point Roger was in the passenger seat and Rebecca was desperately trying to start the car.

"Is there gas?" Benji asked.

"Half a tank," Rebecca said. "Come on!" she said, pressing on the gas. "Start!"

"Hold down the clutch!" Maddy said.

"You think I don't know how to drive?" Rebecca cried. "I've been driving you for thirteen years!"

"Come on, people!" Roger said. "Time for a little teamwork!"

Blam!

Suddenly the family was covered with glass. The old man had blasted a hole in the back window. Now he was running toward them, moving with surprising speed.

"Whenever you're ready, Mom!" Benji cried.

"Hold on!" Rebecca said.

The car finally started. Rebecca fishtailed up the dirt driveway. Benji looked out the shattered back window to see the old man take aim a final time. This time the shot went wide. But then Maddy saw the old woman hustle out of the house, holding a shotgun that was almost a long as she was.

"Duck!" Maddy called.

Blam!

Her shot grazed the car's top.

"Floor it, Mom!" Maddy said.

"The pedal's to the metal!" Rebecca said.

Maddy looked out where the window used to be. The old woman was once again taking aim. As she pulled the trigger, Maddy yelled, "Duck!" again. But the shot missed. Soon her mother had the old Honda barreling up the dirt road that led to the mountain. The woman fired again but was out of range. Maddy faced forward, gasping for breath, trying to calm herself.

"Incredible!" Benji said. "We got their car!"

"Yeah," Maddy said. "And they aren't going to have much luck following us in their old tractor."

No sooner had she spoken than Maddy heard a terrifying roar. She looked over her shoulder just in time to see the old man burst out of the barn on a motorcycle.

"Oh, God!" Maddy called.

"Here he comes!" Benji said.

"Is everyone strapped in?" Rebecca asked.

"Just drive!" Roger said.

Rebecca cut the wheel hard. The car careened around a sharp curve.

"I am getting so sick!" Benji yelled.

"If you puke on me, you're toast!"

"Come on, people!" Roger said. "How about a little togetherness?"

Maddy pressed hard against her brother as the car shot up the road. On one side the mountain rose high; on the other was a steep cliff. Her mom was all concentration, staring straight ahead, one hand on the wheel, the other on the gearshift. She took a sharp turn with a loud screech but stayed on the road and kept going up the mountain.

"Nice, Mom!" Maddy said.

Her mother smiled back in the rearview mirror.

"Bet you didn't know I used to race go karts."

"Really?"

Rebecca winked. Maddy sat back in her seat, impressed, then looked out the back window. Though her mom was pushing the Honda as fast as it could go, the motorcycle was gaining. Kicking up dust and a plume of black exhaust, the old man was soon in range.

"Let's see what you have, Mom," she said. "He's coming!"

Blam!

The man fired but missed. He then wobbled violently but managed to right himself. Rebecca took a turn at ninety miles per hour.

"What's he doing?" she called.

Now mother and daughter were a team. Rebecca the driver, Maddy the navigator.

"He's still coming!" Maddy said. "Move left! Hard!"

Rebecca did as she was told just in time to bump the motorcycle's front wheel, only not hard enough to knock him over.

"To the left again," Maddy said. "Knock him into the mountain."

Before Rebecca could bump him again, the old man took aim and calmly blew out the Honda's left rear tire. The car skidded wildly to the right, then left. Maddy grabbed the door handle to stay in her seat.

Blam!

The old man shot out the right rear tire. Now the car was shooting sparks. Then it got worse. Up ahead, a truck appeared around a curve in the road, coming their way.

"Hold on!" Rebecca called once again.

To Maddy's horror, her mother cut the wheel and crossed lanes, heading directly for the truck.

"Mom!" Maddy cried. "What the hell are you doing?"

"Saving us!"

The truck was coming closer and closer. Maddy closed her eyes as her mother bore down on the truck, daring it to switch lanes. Finally it did, swerving into the other lane at the last possible second . . . directly into the old man.

Boom!

Maddy swung around just in time to see the motorcycle tumbling over the cliff.

"Yes!" Rebecca pounded the wheel. "That's ten years of car pool right there!"

"You kicked serious ass, Mom!" Maddy said. She squeezed her mother's shoulder. "I didn't know you had it in you."

Rebecca patted Maddy's hand and caught her eyes in the rearview mirror. "Thank you, Mads. That means a lot coming from you."

Maddy smiled and collapsed back in her seat. Maybe she should be a little bit easier on her mother. After all, a woman who could drive like that couldn't be all bad.

CHAPTER FIFTEEN

A short time later, Rebecca brought the Honda to a stop on the side of a deserted stretch of road by an unplanted field covered with weeds. The trip down the other side of the mountain had fully destroyed the car's already flat tires, filling the air with the sharp smell of burning rubber.

"Well, so much for driving home," Benji said.

Rebecca took a long look around. There was nothing on the horizon, not even a single house.

"How far from Paris do you think we are?"

"We were knocked out for most of the night," Benji said.

"Great," Maddy said. "We could be anywhere. We might not even be in France anymore."

Roger sighed. It would be nice to know where they were, but it would be even nicer to know that they were safe. Yes, they had escaped the farmhouse and outrun the old couple. But who knew who else had been dispatched to capture them by now? Maybe someone with better aim? Roger glanced worriedly down the road. In the distance, a small speck was moving toward them: a pickup truck. No way was he going to let his family stay in the open as shooting ducks.

"In the ditch, everybody," Roger said. "Now!"

Something had happened to the Hitchcocks over the course of their short, but adventurous, vacation. In their prior life, they had been a group that took their own good disorganized time to do anything or get anywhere. Now they had melded like an elite military unit. With no argument, they flopped into the ditch. Hidden, they watched the pickup come closer, then stop ten yards up the road. A middle-aged man got out, grabbed a suitcase from the backseat, and waved good-bye to the driver. The truck continued on its way, leaving a light trail of dust.

"What next?" Benji whispered. "Do we ask him for help?"

Roger weighed his options. The man was middle-aged, with grayish hair and a slight paunch. He seemed perfectly harmless, perhaps even friendly. Besides, what other options were there? He and his family couldn't lie in a ditch for the rest of their lives.

"Come on," Roger whispered. "Let's find out where we are."

If the man with the suitcase was surprised to see the Hitchcocks rise from the ditch—or that they were covered with soot from their trip up the chimney—he didn't show it. Watching the Americans walk toward him, he nodded hello, then looked back down the road. Roger cleared his throat.

"*Excusez-moi, monsieur?* We're lost."

Once again, the man looked up at Roger. If he understood, he didn't show it.

"Sweetheart," Roger asked Maddy. "How do you say 'lost' in French?"

Maddy shrugged. "Beats me."

"How can you not know that?" Benji said. "You've taken it for five semesters."

Maddy waved her brother off.

"Shush up."

"The truth hurts, huh?"

"*Perdu*," Maddy said.

"Huh?" Benji said.

"'Lost' is *perdu*, all right?"

"See?" Rebecca said. "That wasn't so hard, was it?"

Maddy frowned. It was so like her mother. Hadn't they just bonded in the car? Why did she have to undercut that with a tart comment? Why didn't her mother remember what it was like to be thirteen and keep her mouth shut? Now it was Maddy's duty to say something appropriately irritable in return.

But before she could, the man suddenly replied, but not in French or even English. Instead, his words had a guttural, Eastern European flavor.

The blood drained from Benji's face. "Uh, Dad?"

"Yeah?"

"That sounded Russian."

"It did," Maddy said.

"Well, that's ridiculous." Roger laughed. "I mean, I don't know where we are, but it sure the hell isn't Russia."

"Then maybe we're in Chechnya," Benji said.

"Oh, God," Rebecca said, looking around the barren countryside. "We could be anywhere."

Benji shook his head. "And we don't even have

passports. Which is all my fault."

Rebecca rubbed his shoulders. "It's not your fault, Benji. It's my fault."

Maddy's eyes went wide. It wasn't like her mom to admit a mistake. She must be even more scared than she thought.

"I said call Harry Huberman," Rebecca said.

"No, no," Roger said. "It's me. I never should've suggested this stupid house swap."

Maddy was mystified. An hour earlier her parents were blaming each other; now they were blaming themselves. This was adult behavior? Maybe they just felt guilty about how they had ripped into each other in the old couple's home.

Then Maddy saw something.

"Hey, guys," she said.

"No, no," her mother was saying. "I shouldn't have called Harry Huberman. I'm too trusting."

"On the bus," Maddy said. "Look."

Her mother glanced down the road, then shielded her eyes from the sun.

"Do you see what I see?" Maddy asked.

"I think so . . . ," Rebecca said.

By now Roger and Benji were also watching the bus rumble closer. Then they all saw the sign hanging over the front windshield. It read: *Sofia*.

Benji reached into his pocket and pulled out the paprika-covered note.

"Sofia . . . Bulgaria . . . " He paused. "She's not a person. She's a place!"

The bus pulled to a halt by the side of the road and the door swung open. The middle-aged man picked up his suitcase and walked up the steps. The Hitchcocks hesitated briefly, then followed him on.

"Welcome to Bulgaria. How can I help you?"

It was three hours later. After arriving in Sofia, the Hitchcocks had found their way from a busy bus depot to the American Embassy. Now they were sitting in the cluttered office of a tired-looking agent, a balding man with grayish sideburns that inched down to a messy goatee.

"How can you help?" Roger said. "It's a long story."

"Make that a *really* long story," Maddy added.

"Miles long," Benji said.

The agent sighed. He had been hoping to take a lunch break. A long story was the last thing he needed.

"Let me guess," he said. "You lost your passports?"

Rebecca smiled. "Yes, but that's just the beginning."

The agent frowned. There was something about

Rebecca's tone that told him he'd be lucky to get out for any lunch at all.

"OK," he said with a grumble. "Let's hear it."

In twenty years at the embassy, the agent had interviewed everyone from suspected kidnappers to drug runners. But those cases had been fairly straightforward: bad men and women who often had traceable criminal records. The Hitchcocks' tale was altogether different. As Roger began their story, the agent took assiduous notes without looking up, his expression betraying no surprise. But as the plot thickened, the agent's face began to show confusion, then anger. Was Roger and the family crazy or in true jeopardy? It was hard to tell. When Roger described their perilous escape up the chimney, he finally cut them off.

"Let me see if I got this straight," he said, referring back to his notes. "You came from Chicago, did a house swap in Paris, and found a diary."

"Right," Roger said. "The daughter's diary."

The agent frowned again. "And the whereabouts of this diary?"

"We don't know," Maddy said. "We gave it to Harry Huberman."

The agent twirled an irritated finger through his goatee. "A man you met atop the Eiffel Tower who claimed to be from the American Embassy."

"But was actually a spy," Benji said.

"Right," the man said. "You were then gassed and held hostage by an old lady, who didn't like to let you use the bathroom, and her husband. There was also a dog."

"A really mean dog," Benji said.

"Noted," the man said. "I'll write 'really mean' next to the word 'dog' in my notes."

"Listen," Rebecca said coldly. If there was one thing she hated, it was being patronized. "You might enjoy feeling superior, but we've just been through the wringer. This is serious!"

"I know it's serious," the agent snapped. "That's why I'm missing my lunch to get a thorough record. Tell me more about the Vadims."

"The Vadims?" Roger said.

He was suddenly even more fed up than Rebecca. Hadn't they already explained the situation?

"We've told you already!" Then Roger realized something. He still didn't know exactly why the real Vadims had sent fakes to Chicago. Frustrated with everything, he tried to work it all out. "The Vadims are the family we thought we did the house swap with. But the Vadims who showed up—let's call them the

Chicago Vadims—didn't turn out to be the *real* Vadims, OK? Who knows why? Maybe the real Xavier Vadim knew he was going to steal this vial of MGF and wanted to throw the authorities off track by sending a fake version of themselves to America. All I know is that we somehow ended up in the middle of an international mess and you have to help us!"

"Please," Rebecca said. Suddenly all she wanted was to be in her own house, safe in bed. "Can we please just go home already?"

"America will require your passports," the agent said. "That'll take forty-eight hours minimum."

"Forty-eight hours?" Roger said.

"That's forever," Benji said.

Maddy nodded. "One hundred wall posts in Facebook time."

"Don't worry," Rebecca said. "We aren't waiting any forty-eight hours." She reached under her shirt and pulled out a stack of Euros—the ones she had taken from Madame Vadim's shoe—and painted on her best smile. "Can't we make that a bit quicker?"

"God, Mom," Maddy said. "I thought you were looking a little bit chesty there. Nice."

For the first time since they'd entered his office, the agent smiled, as though he had spent the entire interview waiting for an excuse to call in the cops. "You aren't trying to bribe me, are you, Mrs. Hitchcock?"

"Of course she isn't," Roger said, taking the money. "She was kidding, weren't you, dear?"

Before Rebecca could launch into her own denial, the agent sighed heavily and waved a hand. "Keep your money, all right? I can offer hotel vouchers until your new passports are prepared. That's it."

Rebecca sank back in her seat. "So we're stuck?" she said.

"For two days," the agent said. He glanced icily at Maddy. "Or one hundred wall posts to you."

If Rebecca was resigned to their fate, Roger wasn't—not quite yet anyway. In his view, an American official should do whatever he could to get them home as fast as he could. Also, his little rant about the true identity of the Vadims had gotten him riled up. Suddenly he had to know exactly what was going on— even if it wasn't in his best interest.

"Then how about my phone call?" he said. "Even prisoners get phone calls, right? Are you authorized to let an honest, hardworking American use your phone?"

The agent quietly slid the phone to Roger.

"Dial seven for an outside line. I'll get your vouchers."

The man left the room and Roger picked up the phone.

"Roger," Rebecca said. "Who are you calling?"

"Quiet," he said. "I know what I'm doing."

He punched in their home number. The phone rang twice.

"Hallo?" It was the Chicago Vadim. "Who is this, please?"

Roger knew he should keep his mouth shut. He knew that nothing good could come from confronting the fake version of the man who had tricked him into switching identities. But he couldn't help himself. He needed to vent and he needed to do it now.

"I'll tell you who this is! Roger Hitchcock! The man who owns the house you're staying in. Now who are you—really? I know you're not Xavier Vadim!"

The Chicago Vadim wasn't breaking character. "I am sorry?" he said. "Roger? Are you all right?"

Roger was pacing now. "Please! Explain to me what's going on. You hear me, you piece-of-crap imposter!"

"I have no idea what you're talking about!"

"You have no idea . . . ? *You get out of my house!*"

Roger slammed down the receiver, then looked sheepishly at his family.

"Honey," Rebecca said. "Calm voice."

Roger sighed. "I've lost my calm voice, honey."

Just then the fax machine on the agent's desk began to hum. A moment later an arriving fax began to inch onto the paper tray.

"Oh my God," Benji said.

"What, dear?"

Benji felt his lips go cold. "Look. It's us!"

The appearing document contained the Hitchcocks' passport pictures. Underneath the passport pictures was a group shot.

"That's outside the Eiffel Tower," Rebecca said.

"I told you the Elevator Man was taking our picture," Benji said.

"But what's this all about?" Maddy said. "Why is this guy getting our pictures?"

"Maybe the Elevator Man is alerting all the embassies in Europe to keep an eye out for us," Roger said.

"Yeah," Rebecca said. "To help us get home."

No sooner were the words out of her mouth than the fax finished printing and fell to the floor. Maddy picked it up. The moment she held it up to the light, her skin went cold.

"This isn't good," Benji said.

Maddy had never seen her parents look so pale and lost. It was hard to blame them. The fax had nothing to do with helping them get home. On the bottom of the page, printed in clear bold capitals, were chilling words:

WANTED—FOR ESPIONAGE!

When the embassy agent returned with the family's hotel vouchers, the Hitchcocks were gone, hurrying through streets they didn't know in a city where they didn't speak the language. Before long, they found themselves approaching an outdoor market. Carts selling everything from food to clothing lined an open square. Roger clutched the APB—their "wanted" fax—in his right fist.

"What's going on?" Rebecca asked. "What have we gotten involved in?"

"I don't know, honey."

"It has to be about the MGF," Benji said. "Whatever that is. It was stolen and somehow we're getting framed for it. We find the MGF and we figure this out, right?"

"Right," Roger said. "But keep your eyes down, people. No eye contact, OK? Not with anyone."

Terrified, Maddy did as she was told. What had been a fun adventure had crossed the line into terrifying a while ago. For the time being, she was done thinking about Noah, Grace, or the town pool. It was one thing to be hunted by criminals like Harry Huberman—at least then she had assumed the police were on their side. But now they were being hunted by the government. Did that mean she'd spend the rest of her teen years in a Bulgarian prison, living on saltines and water? How would they ever get home now?

Then Maddy saw it—a vibrant flash of red. Wheeling around, she stared across the square to the outdoor café.

"Maddy!" her mother said. "Did you hear your father? Eyes down."

"Look!"

"I said, eyes down," Rebecca said.

"What is it?" Roger said.

"Yeah, Mads," Benji said. "You look like you've seen a ghost."

"Not a ghost," Maddy stammered. She pointed across the square. "The real Veronique Vadim."

CHAPTER SIXTEEN

S he stood no more than twenty feet away, a thirteen-year-old girl with long red hair, browsing through a cart of books.

"No way," Benji said. "It can't be."

"Yes way," Maddy said. "You didn't sleep in her bed."

"She's got the red hair," Roger said.

"She's the right age," Rebecca said.

"It's her, OK?" Maddy said. "The girl in the pictures and Stephan's painting. Trust me on this."

The family soon got the final proof. As the Hitchcocks

watched, the red-haired girl paid for her paperback, then walked across the square to an outdoor café. At a small table was the rest of her family. The Vadims. A little boy, no more than three, was finishing a bowl of ice cream. The mother, also a redhead, was idly stirring a glass of iced coffee. Then there was Monsieur Vadim himself, browsing through a guidebook.

"The real Xavier Vadim," Roger whispered. "It's him."

Looking at his alter ego was both exhilarating and frightening. The real Xavier Vadim was dark and slim but a tad shorter in real life than his pictures. He wore a light-blue polo shirt and tan slacks.

"Are they following us?" Maddy whispered. "Or are we following them? I'm confused."

"Maybe they can lead us to the MGF," Benji said.

"Or should we call the police?" Rebecca asked.

Roger shook his head. "What are the police going to do? They'll probably arrest us. Our fingerprints are everywhere."

"So we follow them, right?" Benji said.

"Right," Maddy said.

Roger nodded. "Those Vadims are our only chance of figuring out what's going on."

And so a game of cat and mouse began. After the Vad-ims finished their snack, they wandered slowly back up the main street, glancing idly in shop windows. As for the Hitchcocks, they remained far enough away to stay hidden but close enough not to lose the trail. Soon the Vadims made their way to a busy avenue teeming with rush-hour traffic. Across the street was a lavish marble building. The Hitchcocks hunkered down behind a lamppost.

"The Sofia Intercontinental Hotel," Roger whis-pered, looking at his map.

"I bet that's where they're staying," Maddy said.

"Then we'll stay there, too," Rebecca said.

"Come on, guys," Benji said. "They're crossing."

But the rest of the family didn't move fast enough. By the time Benji reached the curb, the light was turn-ing yellow.

"OK, wait," Rebecca said.

Benji's gut told him it was time to channel his inner hero once again. If the Vadims got away now, they would be hard to catch. As the light turned red, he took off into traffic.

"Benji!" Rebecca called.

A cab honked. A truck skidded to a halt. An old man shook a grocery bag. But Benji didn't stop until he had reached the opposite sidewalk.

"Sorry!" he called back. "We can't lose them!"

"Jeez," Maddy said to her parents as Benji hurried past the doorman into the hotel. "The kid steals some car keys and he thinks he's a superhero."

"Yeah?" Rebecca said. "Then he might be the first superhero in history to be publicly spanked by his mother."

Unaware of the possible fate that awaited him, Benji followed the Vadims into the thick of the lobby. As Monsieur Vadim stopped to buy a paper, Benji ducked behind a large plant, heart pounding—not out of anxiety but out of excitement. When Monsieur Vadim stepped out of the newsstand, Benji moved behind a pile of suitcases, then crouched by the side of a decorative fountain. When the Vadims got on the elevator, Benji hurried behind, catching the door with his hand and slipping on at the last second.

"Sorry," he said.

Monsieur Vadim smiled. *"Pas de probleme."*

Benji swallowed hard. It was one thing to track someone from a distance but quite another to confront them face-to-face.

"Ah, merci," he said.

"Your floor?"

This time it was Madame Vadim, an attractive woman with red hair and a kind smile.

With his heart pounding a mile a minute, it was hard to think. The Vadims had pressed "twelve." To find out their room number, he'd have to pick a higher floor.

"Fifteen, please."

Madame Vadim pressed the button for him, and Benji stepped back in between Veronique and Jean-Claude and tried to enjoy the ride. But as the elevator rose, America's latest, greatest spy became more and more nervous. What if Monsieur Vadim recognized him somehow? Looking down, Benji saw Jean-Claude staring up at him. Was he about to be found out by a three-year-old kid? Did he sense that Benji had slept in his Batman bed? Or worn his cape to the opera? Benji gasped. Maybe the spy business wasn't for him after all.

"Jean-Claude!"

It was Madame Vadim.

Benji exhaled sharply. He didn't think it was possible for his heart to beat so quickly and still function.

"*Oui, maman?*"

"*Ne regardes pas.*"

The boy quickly took his eyes from Benji and stared at his feet. The elevator finally stopped—and not a moment too soon. Benji's brow was dripping with actual sweat.

"*Au revoir*," Madame Vadim said.

"*Ah, oui*," Benji stammered. "*Au revoir*."

It was only through an act of sheer will that he was able to press the "open door" button long enough to see the Vadims wander down the hall and stop outside Room 1212. Greatly relieved, he traveled up to fifteen, then pressed "one" to go back downstairs.

"You did it," he told himself, highly pleased with his piece of improvised reconnaissance.

By the time he arrived back in the lobby, Benji's nerves had settled. Now that he was safe, he all but strutted off the elevator.

"Benjamin Hitchcock!"

Benji blinked as though he had expected to be met by a brass band and cheering section, as opposed to one extremely unhappy-looking mother. He had almost forgotten that he had left the family across the street.

"You listen to me, young man! Just because you stole a set of car keys doesn't make you immortal. Did you see that truck? Of course you didn't! Well, it nearly ran you over! Never run across a street like that again. Never sneak across a hotel lobby like a criminal. Or get in an elevator with a family of—of killers!"

Up until the end of Rebecca's little tirade, Benji had been on the defensive. But Rebecca had overplayed her hand.

"Killers, Mom?" Benji said. "Isn't that a bit of an overreaction?"

Rebecca was in no mood to get into a debate on semantics with a nine-year-old.

"Who knows what these Vadims are up to? What kind of people steal vials of things and send fake versions of themselves into the homes of innocent people?"

Now Benji smiled. "That's the point, Mom. Now we can find out. They're staying in Room 1212."

"Bull's-eye, sport," Roger said.

"Guess they didn't kill him, Mom," Maddy said.

"Yeah?" Rebecca turned to Benji. "You run off like that again and I'll do it for them."

A short while later, the Hitchcocks were in an elevator going up to their own room: Room 1412. Since there was no thirteenth floor on the hotel, they would be one floor above the Vadims.

"Tonight we sleep," Roger said. "Tomorrow we spy."

He and Benji slapped five.

"Nice, Dad!"

The elevator stopped at fourteen.

"I don't know about you," Rebecca said as the doors opened, "but the first thing this team member is doing when we get to the room is a no-brainer. I haven't had a hot shower in days."

CHAPTER SEVENTEEN

Early the next morning the Hitchcocks ordered breakfast from room service. After the trays were cleared, Roger slipped into the lobby and purchased four disposable cell phones. Soon after, the family fanned out to their assigned posts. While Roger and Maddy waited in their room, Rebecca and Benji took strategic positions in view of the elevator banks. Benji stood by the concierge's desk. Rebecca crouched behind a giant ficus. Then they waited for the Vadims.

Ten minutes passed. Just when Benji was starting to get bored, he felt a tap on his shoulder.

"Excuse me, *Monsieur*."

To Benji's surprise, he found himself face-to-face with a well-groomed man in an elegant red suit: the concierge.

"May I get you something while you wait?" he asked in perfect English. "A newspaper or perhaps a coffee?"

"Uh, yes, yes," Benji stammered. "Coffee. Extra milk."

"Very good, sir."

The concierge called the dining room to place the order. Eyes on the elevators, Benji moved behind the fountain in the center of the lobby. Five more minutes crawled by. A family of four exited the far elevator—a couple with a girl and a boy. For a moment Benji's heart fluttered: the Vadims! But in seconds, he realized he was wrong. The boy was at least seven and the girl had blond hair. False alarm.

"Your *café*, *Monsieur*."

"Ah, yes. Thank you."

As the concierge turned away, Benji took a sip. It was hotter and much more bitter than he expected. He forced it down with a grimace. As he wiped his chin, his cell phone rang. Benji tapped his Bluetooth.

"What are you doing?"

Benji glanced across the lobby. His mother was staring right at him.

"Are you drinking coffee?"

Caught red-handed, Benji opted for a complete change of subject.

"Do you think the Vadims are staying in for the day, Momma H.?"

"Don't call me that, Benji."

"It's spy talk, Mom. Get with the spirit. And don't forget. I'm Sonny H., OK?"

There was a click on the line. Benji checked his caller ID: his father, conferencing in from the hotel room.

"Got you, Poppa H.," Benji said.

"Still no sign of the Vadims?"

"No," Benji said. "Nothing."

"You might have missed them while you were ordering coffee from the concierge. Your son ordered coffee, Roger."

"Hmmm," Roger said. "Was it good?"

"Pretty good. A little bitter."

"See?" Rebecca said.

"We're getting off the subject," Benji said. "The Vadims. Still no sign of them."

"What do you make of it, wingman?"

Benji scowled. Why couldn't his parents get with the program? "That's Sonny H."

A new voice crackled over the line.

"I still like Baby H. better."

Maddy.

"Chill," Benji said. He paused. "Or I'll post 'Ode to a Noah' on his home page."

Maddy gasped. "You do it. You die."

"You're writing poetry?" Rebecca asked. "How sweet."

"People," Roger said. "Can we keep to the subject: the Vadims."

"Well, what can we do?" Rebecca said. "Maybe they're staying in all day."

Benji sighed. "No one stays in a hotel room all day, Momma H."

Right on cue, the elevator opened. This time the family of four that stepped out was the Vadims—a dark-haired man, an attractive woman, a little boy, and a teenage girl with bright red hair.

"We have a sighting!" Benji said. "I repeat: We have a sighting!"

"Yes!" Roger said.

"How many?" Maddy asked.

"All four!" Rebecca said. "Mrs. Vadim is wearing a

red dress with heels. Mr. Vadim is in a green sweater. I think it's cashmere."

"Thanks for the fashion report, Momma H.," Maddy said.

"They're walking across the lobby now," Benji said.

"Nice work, you two," Roger said.

"Poppa H. and I are ready to go in," Maddy said.

"Wait a second," Rebecca said. "We discussed this, Madeleine. Only your father goes."

"But Benji got to steal the car keys and . . . "

"Your brother is lucky he's still alive! Please don't give me another heart attack. Only your father."

Rebecca clicked off for emphasis, then glanced across the lobby at her son. He took another sip of coffee. Rebecca shook her head and smiled.

Upstairs, Maddy looked at her dad.

"Dad?"

Roger looked guiltily at the door. "I know you want to come, but you heard your mother . . . "

"Yeah," Maddy muttered. "I heard her. I always hear her."

Roger slid open the glass door to the balcony and Maddy followed him out onto it. Across the way was a view of a green park. In the far distance was the golden dome of a cathedral. But at that moment Roger and

Maddy were only interested in what was directly below them: the Vadims' balcony and a door to their room. And inside? Perhaps a clue that would lead them to the true meaning of the MGF.

Roger peered over the edge and gripped the balcony bar with his hands.

"Wish me luck, sweets."

But Maddy still hadn't given up on taking a more active role in the adventure. "Slow down, Dad. Don't you think it'd help to have me with you?"

Roger glanced at his daughter. "Didn't you hear your mom?"

"Yeah, I did. But you know, you're not the boss of me, Dad."

Roger turned around. "I hate to say it, Mads, but actually I am the boss of you. And for four more years according to the great state of Illinois."

"Daddy! Please!"

Roger smiled. "Calling me 'Daddy' won't work either. You're not coming, and that's what's called a nonnegotiable. Now watch out."

Before he could chicken out or Maddy could talk him into letting her come, Roger climbed over the railing. Holding on as tightly as he could, he began to lower himself over the other side so that he was hanging out over the edge of the hotel.

"Wow," he said nervously. "Long drop down, huh?"

He swung himself back and forth twice, then let go and sprawled heavily on the Vadim terrace, landing awkwardly on his side.

"Wow," he said again. "That was farther than I thought."

"Was it?"

Roger blinked. For a moment he thought he was daydreaming. Was Maddy standing right beside him? He blinked again and allowed her to help him to his feet.

"I guess we're not in the great state of Illinois anymore, are we, Dad?"

"How'd you get down so easily?"

By now Maddy was smiling as happily as she had since she had gotten on the plane. "Mom made me take gymnastics for three years. Finally paid off." Before Roger could stop her, Maddy was sliding open the balcony door. "You coming?"

For a split second Roger considered digging in his heels and forcing Maddy to go back to their room. It was an idea he quickly let go. As she had put it, they weren't in the great state of Illinois anymore. Whether he liked it or not, Maddy was becoming a young lady whose opinions and desires could not be ignored.

"Yeah, I'm coming," he said. Then he smiled, thrilled to have company. He had been more frightened than he had realized. "Let's crack this case."

Roger followed his daughter into the room. The lights were off, but there was plenty of sunlight shining through the balcony window to see around. And what Roger and Maddy saw was a mess. A suitcase was open on the bed, with clothes strewn over the pillows. Through the bathroom door, Roger saw a tube of toothpaste open on the floor.

"Boy," Maddy said. "They're bigger slobs than me."

"Just be sure not to touch anything," Roger said. "We don't want to leave any fingerprints or be framed for anything."

"Got it," Maddy said. "I'll take the bedroom and you take the bathroom and closets."

And so the two Hitchcocks got busy, looking around the room, desperately trying to find something—anything—that would let them figure out exactly what they had been dragged into. Though they were looking for the grand prize—some sort of vial filled with the mysterious MGF—all they found instead was more of the Vadims' discarded belongings. Under the bed, Maddy dragged out Jean-Claude's Elmo pajamas and a teddy bear. Behind the night table was a pair of men's underwear and a sweat sock. Behind the TV was a piece of hotel stationery, covered in doodles (again, courtesy of Jean-Claude). Likewise, Roger didn't find anything in the bathroom other than the Vadims' toiletries and an open deck of cards that was covered with leaking shampoo.

"Nothing," he said, walking back into the room.

"Me either," Maddy said.

As if on cue, Roger's cell rang. He tapped his Bluetooth.

"Yes?"

"Just checking in, Roger."

Roger mouthed to Maddy: "Your mother."

"Are you in the room?"

"Yep. Haven't found anything yet."

"Is Maddy safe upstairs?"

Roger winked at his daughter. "Worry not, Momma H., Maddy H. is safe and sound."

"Be careful," Rebecca said. "Don't be too long."

"Over and out, Momma H."

He hung up.

"Thanks, Dad."

Roger smiled. "You owe me one." He looked around the room again. "What next? The closet?"

Maddy stepped over a pile of clothes and pulled open the door. In contrast to the mess in the room, the closet more accurately reflected the Vadims' public persona: every suit, dress, shirt, and pair of pants was perfectly pressed, hung in a neat row.

"I guess they don't let Jean-Claude in here," Maddy said.

Roger brushed his hands over the suits. "They sure brought a lot of clothes. Hmmm . . . Wait."

"What, Dad? Did you find the vial?"

Roger shook his head but smiled. He reached into the inner pocket of a jacket and pulled out four passports. "No, just this."

"Oh my God," Maddy breathed. "The mother lode."

Roger quickly opened the first passport. On the first page was a picture of the man they had seen in the outdoor café. To the side was his name: Xavier Vadim.

"So they are the real Vadims," Maddy said.

"Seem to be," Roger said.

Maddy smiled.

"What?"

"He looks like you, Dad. You know, like the handsome French version."

Roger rubbed a hand through his daughter's hair. To his delight, she didn't flinch. "This is fun, isn't it?

We haven't had daddy-daughter time since the Box Car Derby. Remember? How old were you, Mads, like eight?"

Maddy nodded. "We totally should've won that, Dad."

"Our car was aerodynamically perfect," Roger agreed, and a white business card slid from the passport and fluttered slowly to the floor.

"Whoa, what's that?" Roger asked.

Maddy picked it up, then held it to the light.

"It's the business card for the Bulgarian National Bank," she said. "The main branch."

Before he could answer, Roger felt his cell phone vibrate.

"One second, Mads," he said. "Your mother is getting nervous."

Roger clicked on his Bluetooth.

"This is Papa H."

"Get out of there. Now."

Roger thought it was a joke.

"What?"

Now Benji's voice crackled over the line.

"Get out, Dad! The Vadims are coming back!"

"Now?" Roger said. "They just left!"

"I know," Rebecca said. "But get out of there! I repeat—get out!"

Roger muted the mouthpiece. "We gotta move, Maddy. They're coming back."

"They're already in the elevator," Benji said. "The door just closed."

Roger hung up. "They're in the elevator. Let's move!"

Roger pushed open the glass door to the balcony and ducked outside just as the front door to the room swung open. As her father disappeared outside, Maddy had no choice but to hit the floor and slither on her stomach under the bed. And not a moment too soon. The second she was hidden from view—next to Jean-Claude's pajamas and teddy bear—the lights flickered on and she heard the Vadims—all four of them—enter the room.

She was trapped.

CHAPTER EIGHTEEN

Flat on her stomach, there was nothing for Maddy to do but hold her breath and watch the Vadims' feet moving back and forth across the room. Despite her mediocre French, a few things were clear. First, Veronique was furious—about just what Maddy wasn't yet sure, but whatever it was, her parents were utterly unable to calm her. After a flurry of angry words, Veronique slammed shut the bathroom door and refused to come out. Which is when Jean-Claude decided to use the bed as a trampoline. With each jump, the box spring moved perilously close to Maddy's head. After

Benji's heroics, Maddy had wanted to get into the mix of things, but she never bargained for getting crushed to death by a three-year-old. And there was no hope for a quick reprieve. The Vadims were too preoccupied trying to get their daughter to come out of the bathroom to rein in their overly energetic son.

Terrified, Maddy glanced out from under the bed. Through the balcony window she caught a glimpse of her father, crouched behind a plant. She wanted to scream. What was he doing just sitting there? Shouldn't he barge in and drag her to safety? Punch out the Vadims if that's what it took? Instead, she saw him take out his phone.

What in the world was he doing?

Outside on the balcony, Roger held his phone to his ear. Rebecca answered on the first ring.

"Roger?" she asked. "Are you finished already?"

"Put Benji on," Roger whispered.

"What . . . ?"

"Just do it!"

Inside the room, Jean-Claude was now doing a somersault off the bed onto the floor. Roger prayed that the boy didn't look under the bed.

"What, Poppa H.?" Benji said.

"Listen," Roger whispered. "Don't panic your mother, but I need you to do something."

"Regardez-moi sauter!"

Maddy knew what that meant: "Look at me jump!" Suddenly, Jean-Claude was back on the bed. He jumped high and landed on his rear end right over Maddy's head. The box spring hit her cheek.

"Jean-Claude!" his mother said. *"Arretes!"*

"It's about time," Maddy whispered to herself.

"Non!" the boy yelled.

He jumped again. This time the box spring hit her in the jaw. Enough was enough. Maddy peered out from under the bed. The balcony was ten feet away. If she ran for it, it would force her father to defend her if the Vadims tried to follow.

Whomp!

This time the box spring hit her on the forehead. Maddy eyed the balcony. She'd rather be caught by an angry French family than crushed to death by their hyperactive son.

She would go on the count of three.

On the first floor of the hotel, Benji was running faster than he ever had in his life. He stopped where two hallways intersected and looked to his right and then his left.

Yes!

There it was!

Sprinting down the hall, he all but threw himself at the fire alarm and pulled the lever.

Maddy slithered to the edge of the bed.

One . . .

Two . . .

Three!

A piercing *whoop, whoop, whoop* echoed through the room, loud enough to wake any sleeping guest.

"Mon Dieu!" Monsieur Vadim said. *"C'est l'alarme!"*

"Veronique!" her mother cried. *"Vite! Vite!"*

Maddy stayed put. She heard the bathroom door swing open and then saw Veronique march across the room, followed by her parents.

"Jean-Claude!" his mother said.

Finally the boy jumped off the bed. Then the front door opened and slammed shut. By then Maddy had realized what had happened. In seconds she was out from under the bed and on the balcony.

"You all right, sweets?" Roger asked.

"Fine."

"Good. Now let's get out of here before they realize it's a false alarm."

Roger and Maddy sprinted out the front door and galloped up the stairs to their room. As soon as the fire department discovered that there wasn't a fire, Rebecca and Benji followed. When the family was reassembled back in their room, Benji got out a pad and paper and went online via a hotel computer and called up a French/English dictionary. But safely in their own hotel room, Maddy was able to piece together what she had overheard without any help.

"The real Veronique doesn't want to move to Argentina."

"Argentina?" Roger said.

"Wait, wait!" Rebecca said. "How do you know this?"

Maddy shrugged. "I might have been trapped under their bed and overheard an argument."

Rebecca's eyes went wide in disbelief. She looked at Maddy, then at Roger, then back at her daughter, as if she didn't know who to be angrier at.

"Save it for later, sweets," Roger said. "This is important."

"So is this," Rebecca said. She turned to Maddy. "You told me you were going to stay upstairs. I don't appreciate being lied to."

Maddy trembled from head to foot. Here they were in a hotel room in Bulgaria in the middle of a plot that might very well land them all in prison and her mother had to keep acting like, well, a *mom*. Why couldn't she cut her a break? Congratulate her for risking her life to get valuable information? Why did everything have to turn into a rebuke? Well, if her mother insisted on continuing to play the role of the overbearing parent, Maddy was happy to take the part of the aggrieved daughter.

"Lied to, huh?" she said.

She heard Benji suck in a sharp breath. "Easy, Mads."

But there was no turning back. The words had been itching to get out of her mouth for months now.

"You're the one who is lying to me," she said. "To all of us."

Rebecca was genuinely confused. She knew she was many things, but not a liar. "Lied to? What are you talking about?"

"Don't act all innocent, Mom," Maddy said.

"About what?"

Maddy looked nervously at her dad. "Morganroth and Inker." She turned back to her mom. "I saw you going in there last month."

Rebecca blinked. "So what?"

"So what?" Maddy said. Time to get it all out. "It's a firm that does divorces! Come on! You're going to leave Dad—it's so obvious."

By that time Benji was in the corner with his hands over his face, watching the conversation between two fingers. Maddy's heart was pounding so fast she thought she was going to fall over. But she held her ground as her father turned to her mom.

"Sweetie?" Roger's voice shook. "Is that true?"

Rebecca took his hand. "No. Not at all."

"Don't lie," Maddy said. Her voice was shaking, too—in fact, she was so overwrought, she could barely speak. "I saw you there."

"Yes," Rebecca said. "I was going there to ask for a job, Maddy. A job!"

Benji slowly lowered his hands from his eyes. Roger exhaled.

Maddy felt the blood rushing to her face.

"A job?" she stammered. "Why?"

"For money, Mads," her mother said. "With the price of corn going down the tubes, I thought it was time get back to work. I've been planning to do it for a while now anyway."

Roger smiled and pulled his wife close. "She's a

trained lawyer, you know."

"Yeah," Maddy said. "I know." It was all too much to wrap her head around. "If you don't want a divorce, why do you always seem so annoyed at Dad? Why does everything bug you so much?"

Maddy could tell at a glance that she had hit a chord. Her mother looked almost ashamed.

"Listen," she said finally. "I love your father, OK? Very much." She looked at Roger, then back at Maddy. "No marriage is perfect. That's what marriage is."

"OK, so maybe I'm wrong about the divorce." Maddy paused. It was now or never. If America had been able to claim its independence from Britain, shouldn't she be able to declare hers from her mom? "But you still have to give me my space. I can do things, you know."

Rebecca sighed and brushed a hand through Maddy's hair. "I know. I guess a young lady like you doesn't need her mother anymore."

Maddy was surprised at how sad she suddenly felt. Yes, she had laid into her mother precisely the way she had wanted to. But maybe she had laid it on a little bit too thick.

"No, no," she said. "I still need you." She paused. "Just sometimes."

Maddy let her mother take her into her arms.

Benji rolled his eyes. "Now it's my turn to puke."

For once Maddy ignored him. It felt too good to be held. Out of the corner of her eye, she saw her father smiling.

"Don't be pissed at Dad," she said. "He tried to stop me, but I jumped down to the balcony."

"Don't worry about it," Rebecca said. "I should've let you go."

When mother and daughter finally broke apart, both their cheeks were streaked with tears.

"Is the love fest over?" Benji asked. "Can we get back to business?" He looked at Maddy. "How do you know the Vadims are going to move to Argentina?"

Wiping the tears from her cheeks, Maddy was ready to change the subject to something less emotionally intense.

"Easy," she said.

"Easy?" Rebecca said.

Maddy smiled. *"Je deteste l'Argentine et . . . et je n'y irai jamais.* That's what she said. Which means 'I hate Argentina and I'm never going there.' You know what? I think they just sprang it on her and she's pissed."

"Could be," Roger said.

"And they're moving *demain soir*—tomorrow night."

"Hold on," Benji said. "You heard all of that?"

Maddy nodded. "Yep. And there's more. The exchange of the vial hasn't happened yet."

"Whoa!" Roger said. "Hold on here! You heard that, too?"

Maddy nodded proudly. "I heard the word 'exchange,' anyway. They were talking fast, but I could tell a lot by the inflection in their voices."

By that point Rebecca's eyes were brimming with tears.

"Madeleine Hitchcock!"

For a moment Maddy thought her mother was angry all over again, ready to read her the riot act for sneaking after her father into the Vadims' room.

"What?" Maddy said.

"I just knew it," Rebecca said.

"Knew what?"

Rebecca dabbed her eyes with a tissue. "That you could be good at French!"

As the Hitchcocks huddled in their hotel room, back across the globe in their own home the tall, elegant Frenchman they now knew as the "Chicago Vadim" but whose name was actually Antoine Truffaut wandered into the kitchen and scrolled to a name on his cell phone: Xavier Vadim. A moment later Xavier answered.

"Hallo?"

Antoine paced the kitchen.

"What the hell is going on, Xavier? I knew this plan was too crazy to work."

"What happened?"

"How would anyone believe that I was you and that my kids were your kids? Even an idiot like Roger Hitchcock has figured it out."

Xavier's voice crackled through the line. "Hitchcock has figured it out?"

"Maybe not everything. But he called here—from Sofia! For all I know, he's staying in your same hotel!"

At the other end of the line, Xavier Vadim felt his throat go dry. Roger Hitchcock was in Sofia?

"But what's he doing here? How did he get here?"

"How should I know?"

"Well, did he say anything?"

"No, no. He just ranted that he wanted us out of his house. Of course, I pretended that I didn't know what he was talking about."

"This could be serious," Xavier said. "We have to take care of this Roger Hitchcock."

"Wait a second."

"What?"

In the darkness of the Hitchcock kitchen, Antoine heard a noise. Were they footsteps? Or was his imagination getting the better of him?

"Hallo," Xavier said. "Are you there?"

"Yes, yes. I am here." There they were again. The footsteps. "I think my son is awake. Stay by the phone. I'll call back."

Antoine clicked off and crossed through the kitchen into the dark living room.

"Hello?" he said. "Marcel? Is that you?"

It happened quickly. A flashlight shone in his face, blinding him. Three figures emerged from the curtains, guns drawn. Antoine tried to run but was easily tackled, then handcuffed.

"Je suis innocent!"

"Yeah? Tell me about it!"

If Benji had been there, he would have recognized Jules Camus, the famed Elevator Man, immediately. On a tip from Interpol, he had flown to America to follow a lead.

"Monsieur Antoine Truffaut?" he asked.

"Non, non. *Je m'appelle Xavier Vadim.*"

Jules wasn't buying it. "Do not lie to me, Monsieur Truffaut. I know that you have been best friends with Xavier Vadim for years. I also know that you agreed to use your family as a decoy and come to Chicago posing as the Vadims to throw the authorities off the trail."

"You're crazy!"

The Elevator Man smiled. "Am I? We also know that Monsieur Vadim stole the MGF from his laboratory and is trying to sell it on the open market. So now tell me, Monsieur Truffaut. Where is the MGF?"

The following morning, Roger and Rebecca stood across the street from the Bulgarian National Bank, a solid stone building a block away from their hotel. Dressed in a dignified business suit, hair carefully combed, Roger looked at the front door.

"Whatever we're not supposed to know . . . it's inside that bank." Out of the corner of his eye, he saw Rebecca smiling. "What?"

Rebecca shrugged. "I don't know," she said. "You have this look in your eye I haven't seen in a while. Determination. It's sweet."

Roger smiled, then looked nervously back at the door. Then he put on his best French accent. "*Je m'appelle Xavier Vadim*." He turned to Rebecca. "How do I sound?"

She straightened his lapel. "Just keep the talking to a minimum, OK?"

"OK," Roger said. Another nervous glance at the door. "Well, wish me luck."

Roger got something even better. Rebecca kissed him on the lips. "Go get 'em, Monsieur Vadim."

Roger smiled again, then turned to the bank. Watching him go, Rebecca took out her cell phone and called the hotel room.

Upstairs, Benji answered on the first ring.

"Sonny H. here."

"Is everything all right back there?" his mother asked.

"Fine," Benji replied. "Except we're dying of starvation here, Mom. Room service still hasn't come."

"Still?" Rebecca replied. "That's strange. Well, stay where you are. Your father just went into the bank. As soon as he's out, we'll all eat together."

She clicked off. Benji turned to his sister.

"Dad's inside?" she asked.

Benji nodded. "I hope he does OK."

"Me, too," Maddy said. "But right now I'm focused on my stomach."

"I know, right?" Benji said. "I'm so starving."

"That room service is so not coming," Maddy said. "Come on. I saw a Starbucks downstairs."

Benji blinked. Even with two days of international

espionage under his belt, he still didn't feel comfortable disobeying his parents. "But we promised to stay here."

Maddy frowned—just as he knew she would. "Don't be a wimp, Benji. We run down, get what we want, and come back up. A quick surgical strike."

As his children made their way to the Starbucks, Roger Hitchcock walked down the quiet halls of Bulgaria's largest bank, willing himself to stay calm. A few days earlier he was an underemployed commodities trader. Now he was about to try something he had only seen successfully executed on television shows: steal from a bank safe-deposit box. By this point Roger did have one thing on his side. Two days of intrigue had made him much better at acting calm under pressure. Though his heart was pounding, he grinned amiably at a guard, then approached a clerk.

"Bonjour," he began in his best French accent. "*Je suis ici pour . . . mon* safe-deposit box. . . . *N'est-ce pas?*"

The clerk looked at him blankly.

"I'm Xavier Vadim," Roger said in English. "I need my safe-deposit box."

"Ah, yes," the clerk said. "Your passport, please."

Roger reached into his jacket pocket and pulled out Xavier Vadim's passport. What had Maddy said? Xavier

Vadim was the handsome French version of him? That morning Roger had combed his hair, shaved carefully, and even dabbed on some cologne. Though he didn't look exactly like Xavier Vadim, he hoped that his appearance was elegant enough to pass a quick inspection.

To Roger's relief, the clerk only gave the picture in the passport a quick glance, then stamped something in his entry log.

"Welcome, Monsieur Vadim. If you will follow me, please?"

Roger bowed his head slightly. "*Ah, merci.*"

Maddy and Benji pushed open the Starbucks door and got on line.

"Hey, check it out," Maddy said. "A Frappuccino is the same word in Bulgarian as in English."

Benji was suddenly too nervous to respond—at least not right away. A block away, inside the bank, their father was posing as Xavier Vadim.

"You think this'll work?" Benji asked.

"Maybe," Maddy said.

"Dad has Xavier Vadim's passport, right?"

Maddy nodded. "Right. We found it in his coat pocket."

"So the rest should be easy," Benji said, thinking out

loud. "He gets to the safe-deposit room. And bang! We have the MGF."

"Something like that."

The two children reached the front of the line, where Maddy ordered their drinks and two muffins. Then she and Benji walked to the pickup area. A moment later their food was ready.

"That was fast," Benji said.

"Faster than room service, anyway," Maddy said. "I wonder if they've even showed up yet."

Just then the front door swung open again and a couple walked out. As the door closed, a man in a tan suit caught it at the last second. Though Maddy only saw him out of the corner of her eye, she knew exactly who it was: Xavier Vadim. Behind him was his entire family. Without saying a word, she grabbed Benji's hand and pulled him to the back of the seating area.

"What's going on?"

"Just follow me and keep your head down!"

The guard ushered Roger through a gate, then past a row of offices. Then the guard turned to his left, led him down a flight of stairs, and stopped by a steel door. Roger swallowed hard. Somehow this seemed almost too easy. The guard unlocked the door and led Roger into a room lined with shelves. Soon the guard removed · a safe-deposit box from a shelf and laid it on a table.

"Here it is, Monsieur Vadim."

"Merci," Roger said again.

The guard nodded and left the room. For a moment Roger couldn't believe his good luck. The entire escapade had been effortless! Maybe the Hitchcocks' luck was finally turning?

Sitting down, Roger took his Bluetooth from his pocket and placed it on his ear.

"Hello, Momma H.?"

"Here, Poppa H."

Even Rebecca was getting into the spy business. "I'm inside," Roger said.

"Good news," Rebecca said.

Roger pulled open the lid of the safe-deposit box. Suddenly what had seemed effortless appeared impossible. For tucked inside the safe-deposit box there was another box— one with a ten-digit combination lock.

"Oh, crap," he said.

"What?" Rebecca said.

Then Roger remembered something. The note that Benji had discovered with the word "Sofia" on it . . . wasn't there also a code?

"Patch me through to Benji."

At that point Benji and Maddy were still in the Starbucks, hiding in the back, both working on their drinks. Benji felt his phone vibrate. He saw his father's ID.

"Sonny H. here."

" . . . enji . . . ofia number from Par . . . Have it?"

"What's he saying?" Maddy whispered.

She hadn't taken her eyes off the Vadims since they had arrived. Unfortunately, they had taken their drinks and muffins to a table directly in front of the door. The only thing to do was to lay low until they left.

"I can't understand him," Benji whispered back. "Dad," he said into the receiver. "You're breaking up."

" . . . our Sofia num . . . ," Roger said. "Paprik . . . "

"Paprik?" Benji said. "Do you mean paprika, Dad?"

"What about paprika?" Maddy asked.

"He wants paprika," Benji said.

"No, I want the code!"

Benji finally got it. He feverishly fished the scrap from his pocket and read the number.

07-08-124-977.

"Zero, seven, zero, eight, one, two . . ."

"What?" Roger said.

"One, two, four, nine, seven, seven. . . . Hello, Dad?"

"Yes, I'm . . . ere."

"Did you get it?"

" . . . peat the last . . . num . . . "

"What?" Benji said. "The last one? Is seven. Hello, Dad? Hello?"

"Did he get it?" Maddy whispered.

Benji took the phone from his ear. "Don't know. The line went dead."

Little did Benji know why: In his eagerness to plug in the combination, his father had hung up. With trembling fingers, Roger moved the final sprocket to "seven."

And just like that, it happened.

With a light click the latch flipped open. There it was: a glowing, light-blue liquid in a sealed test tube.

The vial!

La fiole!

The MGF!

Roger pumped his fist, then slipped the test tube into his jacket and closed the box. Now he had one goal: to get out of the bank as quickly as he could. He called for the guard.

"Did you find what you were looking for?" the guard asked.

Roger nodded, doing his best to suppress a smile.

"Yes, I did."

"Very good, sir."

He hurried down the long hallway to the bank's lobby.

"Thank you, Monsieur Vadim," the guard said.

"Of course," Roger replied.

And then, just like that, he was outside. He had done it. Pulled off the impossible. Not bad for a nebbish from Chicago. He looked across the street for Rebecca, eager to show off the grand prize, but to his surprise she was nowhere in sight.

Probably at the Starbucks, he thought, and headed down the block, so happy it was all he could do to keep from skipping. Still, he made sure to walk—best not to look suspicious. There would be plenty of time to celebrate later.

And then his phone rang. It was Benji's caller ID. He couldn't wait to tell him the good news.

"Hey there, sport!" Roger all but shouted into the receiver. "I did it. I got the vial!"

At that precise moment Roger's celebration officially ended. The voice at the other end chilled him.

"And I have your children, Roger Hitchcock."

Roger stopped, heart thumping. "Who . . . who is this?"

Vadim laughed. "The man you traded lives with."

"Xavier Vadim?"

"I found your children in the Starbucks. Imagine my surprise when I was drinking a latte and I overheard someone shouting the combination to the vault inside the safe-deposit box. Now, you have something that belongs to me."

"Please," Roger said. "Don't hurt my kids."

It was then that Roger heard a click. He glanced at his phone. Call-waiting. The name on the ID: Rebecca. Did he dare take the call?

"Hurt your kids?" Vadim said. "Give me the MGF and I won't have to."

"Hey, listen," Roger said. "This is awkward, but, well, just hold on a second."

Roger switched lines.

"Now listen, Becs," he said. "Don't freak out."

Instead of his wife, a familiar voice crackled over the line. "I have your wife, Mr. Hitchcock."

Roger felt like falling over. He leaned against a store window like he'd been gut punched. "Oh my God. Harry? Harry Huberman?"

"The very same."

"What . . . what are you doing here?"

"The same thing as you, Mr. Hitchcock. Looking for the MGF. I'm willing to trade it for your wife."

Roger inhaled deeply.

"You have my *wife?*"

"Don't worry. She's perfectly healthy." He paused. "For now."

Roger forced himself to stand up straight and think.

"Listen, hold on a sec, OK?"

He switched lines back to Monsieur Vadim.

"Where do you want to meet?"

Vadim's voice was level, betraying no emotion. "There is a deserted monastery forty miles north of Sofia. We meet there at six. You take the bus and come alone."

"At six," Roger repeated. "Right. Alone. Done."

With that, Roger took a deep breath. He had one more thing to do. He clicked back to the other line.

"Do not put me on hold ever again, Mr. Hitchcock."

"I'm sorry," Roger stammered. "It was my kids."

"I do not care about your kids, Mr. Hitchcock. How do I get my MGF?"

Roger couldn't believe what he was about to do— but what were his options?

"There's a monastery, due north of the city. Meet me there at six. You give me my wife and I'll give you your MGF."

With a click the line went dead. Roger found himself standing on a crowded street, all alone, in a strange city. Distraught, Roger sank slowly to his knees, his face pressed against the storefront window. Which is when he noticed something. He was looking at a display of toothbrushes, aspirin, and mouthwash.

He was standing outside a drugstore.

Before him was a bottle filled with light-blue mouthwash—the same color as the MGF.

Roger stood up slowly. Did he dare? It was crazy. Then again, what other choice did he have? With a quick glance over his shoulder to make sure he wasn't being watched, Roger hurried into the store.

CHAPTER NINETEEN

Early that evening Roger Hitchcock sat in the back-seat of a public bus that was snaking its way up a winding road toward the monastery. Behind him the lights of Sofia were receding rapidly into the distance. Roger looked out the window and tried to breathe. Had he really done it? Promised to hand over the MGF to two different people? Then again, what other options had he had? He couldn't go back to the embassy—not with an APB out accusing him of espionage. Besides, his gut told him that if he brought along a troop of possibly trigger-happy agents, it would lead to disaster.

No, his only chance to retrieve his wife and kids was to go in alone.

Even so, he wished there had been another way. . . . Roger reached into his pocket and took out a bottle of mouthwash and a small test tube that he had purchased at the drugstore. The mouthwash was light blue, the precise color of the MGF. Working carefully, Roger poured a bit of the mouthwash into the empty vial. Then he reached into his other pocket and pulled out the real vial of MGF. The similarity was remarkable. No one would be able to tell the difference. At least he hoped not. The lives of his family depended upon it.

While the bus carrying Roger Hitchcock moved slowly away from Sofia, his children sat on the stone floor of an abandoned sanctuary inside the deserted monastery. Rows of empty pews filled the chapel. A large fresco of what looked like a saint was painted on the wall over an old church organ.

Benji nodded up at his sister. "I wonder if that thing still plays."

Maddy shrugged. The last thing on her mind at the moment was music.

"Who cares?"

"I do. I bet Beethoven's *Pathétique* would sound unreal

in this place." Benji took in the enormity of the old cha-pel. "The ceiling goes up forever. Killer acoustics."

Maddy didn't answer. Across the way sat Veronique and Jean-Claude Vadim. On a pew in the second row, their parents were talking heatedly. Though their French was far too rapid for her to understand completely, from the few words she was able to catch—*stupide*, *fiole*, and *incroyable*—Maddy got the distinct impression that they were even more scared than she was. Xavier Vadim looked like a chemist, not a spy. And Beatrix Vadim's concerned frowns reminded Maddy strongly of her mother. Though she knew she should be terrified, Maddy couldn't imag-ine either Vadim parent actually harming her.

Maddy tried to catch Veronique's eye. The French girl looked away unhappily. Maddy sighed and stared at the ceiling. Benji was right—the acoustics were prob-ably phenomenal. She was about to say something to him about it—just to make some conversation—when she heard a light thud. To her surprise, Benji and little Jean-Claude had started a game of catch with a rubber ball.

Maddy looked back at Veronique. Again, the girl wouldn't meet her eyes. Maybe she needed a friend. The few days in Paris had given Maddy a small degree of confidence about her French. If Benji could play catch with Jean-Claude, why couldn't she try to strike up a conversation with Veronique? She thought a minute to make sure she got the grammar right, then cleared her throat.

"*Vous ne voulez pas aller à l'Argentine.*"

Veronique looked at her, betraying no emotion. To Maddy's surprise, when she finally answered, it was in English.

"How do you know I don't want to go to Argentina?"

"Not with Stephan back in Paris you don't."

Maddy enjoyed the surprise that flashed over Veronique's face.

"How do you know about Stephan?"

Maddy smiled.

"In his apartment," she said. "He painted you."

Veronique sat up. *"Moi? Sérieusement?"*

"Yes, seriously." All of a sudden she felt like Veronique was a kindred spirit. "It's beautiful, too. Stephan's crazy for you, Veronique."

"But how did you get in his apartment?"

"Through the skylight. Really long story."

The girls were quiet for a moment. Maddy thought of the beautiful painting, then thought sadly of Noah Willis. Compared to a romantic Parisian painter, he seemed so ordinary. Even so, she couldn't think of him without a distinct lump in her throat.

"You know," she said. "There's a guy I like, too."

Veronique raised her eyebrows. "Oh?"

Maddy nodded. "My best friend, Grace, is probably rubbing suntan lotion on his shoulders right now."

Veronique shuddered. *"Oh, Mon Dieu! C'est terrible!"*

As Maddy laughed, Veronique's parents got up from the pew. Apparently their discussion was over. Monsieur Vadim walked grimly up the aisle of the chapel, heading outside, while Madame Vadim approached the children.

"Don't worry," she said. "Your parents are coming for you. It will be over soon."

Benji looked up from his game of catch with Jean-Claude.

"You do realize that in our country, this is called kidnapping."

To Maddy's surprise, Veronique's mother shook her head sadly. *"Oui.* In our country, it is called kidnapping, too."

Ten miles away on a deserted airfield, Harry Huberman clutched Rebecca by the elbow, pushing her toward a military helicopter. His limo driver followed two paces behind, holding an AK-47.

"Are you ever going to tell me who you are?" Rebecca asked Huberman. "Are you even American?"

Harry flashed the winning smile that had charmed her when they first met. What had once seemed dashing now seemed strangely macabre. Rebecca shivered.

"I'm as American as baseball, apple pie, and subprime mortgages," Huberman said. "I'm just a businessman. A security consultant."

"What kind of security consultant?"

The helicopter's propellers began to spin. Huberman shouted over the roar. "I secure transactions, Mrs. Hitchcock. I've been contracted by a Chinese energy corporation to make sure a certain deal gets done."

"And even at the Eiffel Tower," Rebecca said. "You were following us. Why?"

"Because I never trusted Vadim. He promised to sell my client the MGF, then turned around and sold it to a higher bidder. Now I'm back to get my client what is rightfully his."

They reached the helicopter.

"Inside!" Huberman shouted.

With a bodyguard behind her, Rebecca had no choice. She climbed the ladder and took a seat in the back next to an elegantly dressed sixty-something Chinese man in a suit—clearly Huberman's client.

"Meet Mr. Chen," Huberman said, following Rebecca into the copter.

The man grunted; Rebecca nodded back. With the bodyguard and Huberman in the front seat, the pilot closed the door. As she felt the helicopter lift from the ground, Rebecca had never been more terrified.

"You do realize that we have nothing to do with any of this!" she shouted.

Huberman turned and met her eyes. There was no hint of a smile. "Unfortunately, you have everything to do with it, Mrs. Hitchcock. Your husband has the MGF. Let's just hope he doesn't try anything stupid."

CHAPTER TWENTY

For a brief, blissful second Roger was back in the hotel with Rebecca and the kids. Instead, he opened his eyes to the craggy face of a sixty-something bus driver with garlic breath.

"Monastery," the man grunted, then motioned to the door.

Roger blinked. Had he really dozed off? Apparently. He looked out the window. The sun was just beginning to set behind the mountains, casting an eerie orange glow on a once grand but now decaying stone structure that rose as if from out of nowhere atop a cliff.

"Out!" the man barked.

Roger did as he was told. The moment Roger set his foot on the dirt road, the driver shut the doors and sped off. Roger was overcome with a feeling of deep dread. What had he been thinking? That he could outwit organized criminals on his own? Perched atop a bluff, the monastery looked like nothing less than a haunted castle—the type of place from which innocent people didn't escape with their lives.

Roger wheeled around and looked pleadingly down the road, almost as if willing the bus to return and take him back to Sofia or, better yet, transport him to an alternate reality where he and his family had never agreed to go on a house swap to Paris at all. A reality where he had let Maddy hang out by the pool to spend her summer engaged in such meaningful pursuits as drinking an excess of soda and drooling over Noah Willis's triceps. A reality where he had happily paid for Benji to go to computer camp. But would that really have been better? Certainly, it would have been *safer*. But a bland, unadventurous summer held its own perils. Maddy would have graduated from her days at the pool with a great tan but an even worse attitude. Benji would have come home from camp smarter but quite possibly even stranger. And how would he and Rebecca have fared all summer without the kids to keep them busy?

Roger shuddered. No, the current situation was terrible—no question about it. But the family had benefited, hung together, been tested. Assuming he could get them home alive, the family Hitchcock would most certainly be the better for it. And so when Roger took another look up at the monastery, it was with a steely determination. Yes, it was scary. He might screw up even worse than he had at Yosemite. He might even die. But he had to give it his best shot—to prove, if not to the world, then at least to himself and Rebecca, Maddy, and Benji that nice guys could come out on top.

"Bring it on, Harry Huberman!" he said to himself. "Come on, Xavier Vadim! You don't scare Roger Hitchcock!"

With those words, Roger started up the path, hiking steadfastly up a narrow trail that snaked along the side of the mountain by a fifty-foot drop-off and soon dead-ended at the edge of a sheer cliff. One hundred feet overhead stood the old monastery, still and deserted. To climb up was an impossibility. But to Roger's right stood an old funicular, a small metal cabin that moved up and down the side of the cliff like an elevator. Roger looked inside and quickly discovered a lightly rusted control panel. Pressing a dull green button, he waited for the motor to catch. When it didn't, he pressed the button again. Still nothing. Roger gave the funicular a light kick, stepped back outside, and looked again for a path up the cliff. For a brief second he imagined pulling himself up the side by one of the low-hanging vines. He even gave one of the vines a tug to see if it was secure.

Then he heard it—the grinding of an old motor. A lone bulb atop the funicular lit up. So the old contraption worked after all. Roger smiled grimly. Obviously, someone up top was waiting for him. But who? In any case, this time when he pressed the green button the funicular began to rise. Hopping on, Roger watched the ground spread out beneath him as the monastery walls grew larger and larger above him until the funicular came to a sudden halt. A gate clanged open and Roger walked onto a lawn of uncut grass. To his left stood a chapel with a courtyard. To his right was what appeared to be an abandoned dining hall or theater.

"Hello?" Roger called.

His voice echoed back at him. Roger waited, willing himself to stay calm. But it was hard when everything was so still. Someone had started the funicular, but who? There was no sign of another soul—not the Vadims, Harry Huberman, or, most important, his family.

"Hello?" Roger called again. "I'm here."

A shape moved out of the shadows. Roger instinctively took a step back as Xavier Vadim walked toward him across the courtyard.

"Roger Hitchcock," he said.

Roger took a step toward his alter ego.

"So we finally meet face-to-face, after all those emails this spring," Roger called. He paused. "That was you I was emailing with, wasn't it?"

Xavier Vadim was in no mood for small talk. He stopped ten feet away.

"Where is my MGF, Mr. Hitchcock?"

Roger was determined to hang tough. "Where are my children?"

Vadim took a step forward. Though Vadim was doing his best to appear threatening, Roger suspected that he was as uncomfortable playing the part of a heavy as Roger was himself.

"Don't mess around with me, Hitchcock," he said. "I hold the cards here!"

"No, Xavier," Roger said. "I hold the cards! You don't see your MGF until I see my children. Where are they?"

"Nearby," Vadim said. "And safe. Last I heard, our daughters were talking." Vadim allowed himself a small smile. "About boys."

Roger grinned. Suddenly the two men weren't adversaries but fathers, both doing their best to navigate the perilous waters of raising a teenage daughter.

"Good," he said. "Let's make a deal and wrap this up."

Roger had been so focused on Xavier Vadim that he hadn't heard the approaching helicopter—at least not at first. Now he and Vadim looked up at the same time. The large green machine was descending rapidly, kicking up wind and dust.

"Who is that?" Vadim asked.

Roger didn't answer. Rather, he watched as the helicopter approached. Harry Huberman was next to the pilot and his limo driver. In the back was someone else—another man, Roger thought, possibly Asian—sitting next to his wife.

"Rebecca!" Roger shouted.

He didn't think she heard him. But as the copter touched down, their eyes met. After years of marriage, Roger could read her face like a secret code. A single glance communicated love, pride, fear, and a healthy dose of "don't do anything dumb."

"I thought I said to come alone," Vadim said, walking to Roger's side.

"You're a married man, Vadim," Roger said. "You should understand. I didn't have a choice."

The pilot cut the engines. As the propellers slowed, Huberman emerged from the helicopter, gripping Rebecca by the arm. Again, Roger caught her eye. Closer, she looked terrified. As for Harry Huberman, he looked furious.

"What is he doing here, Hitchcock?" he shouted, pointing to Vadim.

Roger drew in a deep breath. If there was ever a time to bring out his inner hero, this was it.

"I figured it was time for a summit."

With that, the Asian man emerged from the helicopter, carrying a leather briefcase.

"This is my business associate, Mr. Chen," Huberman said. "I tracked down the MGF for him."

"Then everyone can leave here happy," Roger said. "You and Mr. Chen will get your MGF and Vadim will get his money. All I'll need is my family back and we'll be on our way to Chicago like nothing ever happened."

Roger pulled out the test tube of MGF and held it up. Huberman nodded.

"Very good, Mr. Hitchcock," Huberman said. "You have a deal. Your wife for the MGF."

Vadim had different ideas. "No trades until I get

my money! The MGF is mine!"

Harry Huberman smiled. If Roger hadn't known differently, he would have thought Huberman was the same charming man he had met atop the Eiffel Tower.

"Circumstances have changed, Mr. Vadim. We don't need to pay you anything at all. Hitchcock has the MGF, which he will trade for his wife, no money required."

Roger sucked in a sharp breath. Had he misplayed his cards?

"Wait a second, Huberman. It's more complicated than that. You see, Vadim has my kids."

At that, Vadim took a pistol out of his pocket. In a flash, the bodyguard had his AK-47 pointed at him. There was a deadly pause. No one moved.

"Don't do anything stupid, Xavier," Huberman said finally.

But Vadim was beyond acting rationally. Shaking with terror and frustration, he kept the gun poised straight at Huberman's head. "I will get what was promised me!"

For a moment no one moved.

"Just give us the vial, Roger," Huberman said slowly. "And no one gets hurt."

Roger was in too deep to take the easy way out now.

Trembling, he held out the vial.

"I have to know where my kids are or this thing shatters!"

Which is where things stood for another second that felt like an hour when the bold opening chords of Beethoven's *Pathétique* Sonata filled the courtyard. Stunned, Rebecca turned to face the chapel.

"Benji!" she screamed.

"It's him!" Roger said. "He's inside."

Vadim blinked, obviously as surprised as the Hitchcocks to be hearing the music. But the bodyguard was too professional to break his concentration. The very instant Vadim looked away, he shot. Vadim cried out, wounded in the arm.

Now that he knew exactly where his children were being held, Roger had nothing more to gain where he was.

"You want your MGF?" he shouted. "Take it!"

He threw the vial into the air with all of his might. While it was still on the way up, he grabbed Rebecca's hand.

"Run!" he cried. "The chapel!"

They took off at a mad sprint. Huberman dove for the falling vial and managed to bat it into the air before it hit the ground. Mr. Chen himself lurched to his left and caught it in his fingertips. The businessman rose quickly to his feet and nodded toward the Hitchcocks.

"Let them go," Huberman said. "We have what we came for. Let's test the MGF."

Roger and Rebecca pushed through the door into the chapel. The powerful strains of the Beethoven sonata echoed off the walls, filling the space with beautiful overtones.

"Benji!" Roger cried, and sprinted down the aisle toward the organ. Maddy jumped up from behind a pew.

"Mom!"

"Maddy!"

Mother and daughter fell into each other's arms.

"They were holding us here."

"Did they hurt you?"

"No, no. We're fine."

Benji looked out from behind the organ.

"Dad!" he called.

"Wingman!"

A moment later the whole family was hugging and kissing, reveling in each other's company. Out of the corner of his eye, Roger saw an elegant woman step out of the shadows.

"Wait! Who is this?"

"It's cool, Dad," Maddy said. "This is Madame Vadim. Jean-Claude and Veronique are up front. We've been hanging together."

Rebecca looked at Madame Vadim.

"Your husband is outside," she said. "And hurry. He's been shot in the arm."

Without another word, Madame Vadim sprinted for the back of the chapel. Once she was gone, Roger turned to his family.

"OK, team Hitchcock. Time to move!"

Maddy called down the aisle. *"Au revoir, Veronique."*

"Bon chance, Madeleine."

"Wait," Rebecca said. "You two became . . . *friends?*"

Maddy nodded. "I told her all about how Stephan is hot for her."

"That's sweet," Roger said. "But we've got to motor!"

The family ducked out a side door and ran back to the funicular.

"Why so fast?" Rebecca said. "You gave them the MGF, right?"

Roger stopped, winded, scared, but strangely exultant. He grinned mischievously. "Well, not exactly."

Rebecca's eyes went wide. "What?"

"What'd you give them then, Dad?" Benji asked.

Roger shrugged. "Listerine."

"Listerine!" Maddy said. "Where's the MGF?"

Roger held up his leg. "Strapped to my ankle."

Unfortunately, as Roger showed his family what he had done, Harry Huberman demonstrated that he had figured it out as well. Just then the Hitchcocks heard his voice echo through the empty monastery.

"Find them!" he cried. "Find those Hitchcocks!"

CHAPTER TWENTY-ONE

The Hitchcocks ran for their lives, wildly improvising with every step. Seeing that the direct route to the funicular was blocked by Harry Huberman, Mr. Chen, and their bodyguard, Roger led the family back through the side door of the chapel. And just as Huberman burst in behind them, Benji noticed a stairwell.

Soon the family found itself running down a haphazard series of underground tunnels with damp walls and low ceilings. It was the kind of place that Benji imagined was used to film horror movies. Around each corner, he expected to come upon a skeleton or a family of hungry rats. But either would have been preferable to what was following them. Turning down a wide hallway, Benji heard the unmistakable sound of machine-gun fire.

"Oh, God!" he said.

"We're so going to die!" Maddy called.

Rat-a-tat-tat!

"Just keep moving!" Roger cried.

"Where to?" Rebecca asked.

Before them was a path that appeared to lead even farther into the bowels of the monastery.

"This way!" Maddy said.

The family sprinted behind her.

"It's no use, Hitchcocks!" Huberman called down the long corridor. "We've got you trapped."

Rat-a-tat-tat!

The bullets hit the top of the tunnel, sending down a spray of dirt and dust. Rebecca slipped hard in a puddle. Roger dragged her to her feet.

"Keep moving!"

Out front again, Maddy saw her only option was a narrow stone stairway that descended quickly into the darkness.

"Follow me!"

Feeling the walls for balance, the family went down,

down, down into the underbelly of the monastery. Soon the stairway bottomed out into a pitch-black hall-way. The air smelled damp and old.

"I can't see a thing!" Rebecca called.

"Cell phones, everyone," Benji said.

"Cell phones?" Roger asked.

Benji flipped his open, emitting a dim light.

"Good call, wingman!"

A moment later each Hitchcock had their phone open, producing just enough light to make out a twisted path of dirt walls and low ceilings. A thin line of water ran down the middle of the tunnel.

Taking the lead, Benji followed the path, first to the left, then back to the right. Then the path widened slightly. Maddy gasped.

"Is this . . . a dungeon?"

Benji held up his cell phone, illuminating a row of cells with rusted metal bars.

"Sure seems it," he said.

Then he gasped. Had he brushed against an actual skeleton?

"Keep moving!" Roger said.

A rat—a big one, too—scurried across Maddy's feet.

"Ahhh!"

Up ahead, Benji gasped again. There was another skeleton, this one sitting upright in a chair, smiling, almost as if watching people go by from its prized seat on the front porch of a lovely house.

"Hitchcocks!" Benji shouted. "Let's move it!"

Directly ahead, the route split. One path went straight, the other veered to the left and up. Benji felt his mother come up behind him.

"Where to?" she asked.

"Up!" Benji said. "Let's get out of here."

He took the lead again. To the sound of a not-so-distant *rat-a-tat-tat*, the family sprinted up the tunnel. The path soon intersected another. By now Benji had a gut feeling about how to get out.

"This way!"

The family put their fate into Benji's hands and followed. As the path rose upward, a stream of light flashed down from above.

"Hurry!" Benji said.

He led them up a narrow set of stairs. Soon the family spilled out of an underground tunnel to the front yard of the monastery. Bull's-eye!

The funicular was twenty feet away.

"Go! Go!" Roger yelled.

Benji and Maddy took the lead, sprinting like

they never had before while Rebecca hurried behind as quickly as she could. Once his family was on the funicular, Roger stopped at a control panel by the edge of the cliff.

"Take us down, Dad," Maddy yelled.

If only it was that easy. On the way up, Vadim had worked the controls. But there were a good ten switches on the panel. Which one started the thing? With nothing else to do, Roger started madly flipping switches.

"Come on," he shouted. "Start!"

A round of gunfire pierced the air. Mr. Chen, Huberman, and the bodyguard burst out of the tunnel.

"Press them all!" Maddy cried.

Desperate, Roger ran his hand across the entire control panel. Then, a miracle—the motor turned over.

"It's moving!" Rebecca yelled.

More than moving—moving quickly.

"Jump on!" Maddy said.

Rat-a-tat-tat!

More machine-gun fire. Here came the bodyguard, traveling like a powerful locomotive, gun raised.

"Jump!" Benji said.

Roger leaped into the air just in time to grab on to the edge of the funicular by his fingertips. Slipping fast, he felt the strong hands of his family grab on to his wrists and pull with all their might. Roger slithered his way into the funicular and rolled onto his back, panting, as exhausted and helpless as a fish who has been brought onto a boat after a long and furious fight.

"We did it." He gasped. "We're free!"

Whomp!

The family froze. Had Roger spoken too soon?

"What the hell was that?" Rebecca asked.

"I'll tell you what!" Benji cried. "Someone jumped on!"

Then came gunfire ripping through the funicular roof.

"It's the bodyguard!" Roger pushed his family against the wall. "Stay here!"

With that, he began to shinny up the side of the funicular.

"God, Daddy! What are you doing?"

Roger was acting on pure instinct. With a primal shout, he grabbed the bodyguard's leg and pulled for all he was worth, dragging the heavy man onto the funicular floor with another loud whomp. But the moment he hit the metal, the bodyguard was up on his knees, gun aimed. Roger pushed the barrel aside at the last possible second, and the burst of fire rocketed against the cliff, shredding loose vines. Roger glared down at his assailant.

"No one shoots at my family!"

He pulled up hard on the gun, flipping the bodyguard backward and off the funicular. With a helpless scream, the man fell fifty feet to the rocks below. Roger turned to his family, bursting with a sort of nervous exultation. Had he really done it? Saved them all from the clutches of a certified killer?

"Oh my God!" Maddy said. "Daddy! You're the Terminator!"

"A terminator who almost wet his pants," Roger said.

"Who cares?" Benji said. "You did it!"

Roger looked at his wife. Her face was marked with equal parts disbelief and pride. As Roger took a step toward Rebecca, arms outstretched, a grinding whirr filled the sky above them. Roger looked up. The helicopter!

"Not over yet, Hitchcocks," he said. "Everybody out!"

By that point the funicular was five feet from the ground. Maddy and Benji jumped off easily. Rebecca fell hard but rolled to her side and stood. Roger went last. Hitting the ground, he grabbed the bodyguard's gun and aimed at the helicopter. Huberman was at the controls.

"It's over, Harry!" Roger called.

He pulled the trigger.

Disaster. He was out of bullets.

Then they heard Huberman's voice.

"Come in, Roger. We need to talk."

Roger panicked. Where was it coming from?

"There, Dad," Benji said.

Roger looked down. Ten feet away, the bodyguard's body was sprawled out on the rocks, neck broken. Huberman was speaking through his radio. Roger picked up the headset and pressed it to his ear.

"Is that you, Huberman?"

"Give me the test tube, Hitchcock."

Roger was now grimly determined. "You're going to have to rip it out of my bare hands."

Huberman laughed. "Nothing would please me more."

Roger saw at once what he had to do: Destroy the MGF. And there was only one way. On the path up he had passed a fifty-foot cliff. Roger took off at a sprint.

"Roger!" Rebecca called. "No!"

But Roger was a man on a mission. So was Huberman. He maneuvered the helicopter expertly and was soon flying directly after Roger, the lights of the chopper bearing down on Roger's back.

"Don't throw the MGF!" Benji yelled, running behind. "We don't even know what it is!"

"He's right," Maddy said, sprinting as well. "It might blow up the whole country!"

Roger didn't care. He had seen a way to end Harry Huberman once and for all. Up ahead was a tangle of what looked like telephone wires. If he could only get Huberman to fly into it . . .

Holding the MGF over his head, Roger ran for the edge of the cliff. Huberman swooped closer, laughing triumphantly. He lowered the helicopter's front and flew low and hard.

"Duck!" Maddy cried.

Roger did—and not a moment too soon. The chopper swooped low, narrowly avoiding taking off his head. Huberman calmly circled back around and spoke into his headset.

"You think you can outmatch me, Roger Hitchcock? You're nothing. A stain on my windshield."

Roger was fully invested in his new self—a brave, almost stupidly courageous man who wouldn't back down from anyone or anything. He had been through too much. Just then he heard a high-pitched buzzing—

the hum of wires. He looked over his shoulder. He was right. Telephone wires.

Roger wheeled back around to face the helicopter. Standing now at the very edge of the cliff, he held out the vial.

"Come and get me, Huberman!"

The great green machine rocketed straight toward his head. Once again, Roger ducked at the last second.

"Give it up, Roger," Huberman said. "It's over."

He had spoken too soon. In seconds his propellers were entangled in the telephone lines. Sparks flew into the air. Then the nose pointed down and the chopper smashed into the ground and exploded. Thrown backward, Roger found himself staring up at the sky.

"Daddy!" Maddy called. "Are you OK?"

"Speak to me!" Rebecca said.

"Come on, wingman," Benji said.

Roger was overcome. Tears flowed down his face—tears of joy and relief. He looked up at his family, realizing as if for the first time how much they meant to him.

"I love you guys," he said. "I really, really love you guys."

Then a ghost rose from the helicopter wreckage. At least that's what it looked like to Roger—a ghost who was holding a dismembered helicopter blade, wielding it like an oversized machete. By the time Roger realized that the ghost was actually the still living and breathing Harry Huberman, the killer was already swinging for his throat.

"Daddy!" Maddy called.

Benji threw himself at Huberman's knees. The man went down hard but lurched back up to his feet.

"You don't decide when it's over, Hitchcock!" Huberman said. His face was matted with blood. The arm not holding the helicopter blade was clearly broken. "I decide when it's over!"

Huberman raised the blade high.

Then came the gunshot. Huberman clutched his chest, looking for a split second as handsome as he had atop the Eiffel Tower, then fell hard to his right, dead. As one, the Hitchcocks looked back up the hill. There stood Xavier Vadim, holding a gun, his family by his side. Before Roger could so much as wave, a squad of Interpol agents burst out of the woods, guns trained on the Vadims. A split second later a bright light pierced Roger's eyes. Four more agents stepped out of the trees, pistols drawn. The leader stepped forward.

"Where is the MGF, Mr. Hitchcock?"

As Roger opened his hand, revealing the small glass test tube, he couldn't help but laugh.

"All of this for a little jar of light-blue liquid. Crazy world, huh?"

CHAPTER TWENTY-TWO

"*Monatomique glycolinate formule.*"

It was a day later. The Hitchcocks sat in an office at Interpol in Paris, across from Benji's old friend the Elevator Man, Jules Camus.

"Otherwise known as MGF," Jules went on.

"But what was it?" Benji asked.

Now that Benji knew Jules was a good guy, he found his pierced eyebrow cool, not scary.

"Part of a top-secret project of the French government," Jules explained. "Synthetic fuel made in a lab."

"I get it," Maddy said. "The answer to the world's energy crisis."

"Exactly," Jules said. He looked at Rebecca. "You have a bright girl here."

Rebecca nodded. "I know."

Maddy couldn't hold back a smile. It wasn't often that she was the one who was called bright.

"In any case," Jules said, "Vadim was selling it to the highest bidder. He and his accomplice, Monsieur Truffaut, have confessed everything."

"And the whole house swap thing?" Roger said. "It was somehow part of their plan?"

"Ah, yes!" Jules said. "Truffaut learned that Vadim was planning the swap, so he approached the professor with the idea that Vadim steal the formula while the Truffauts used the house swap as a diversion. Then they would all begin new lives together in Buenos Aires."

Benji smiled. "Which wasn't quite the way it went down."

Jules nodded. He looked at each of the Hitchcocks. "We owe you all a great debt. If this MGF had fallen into the wrong hands, the balance of world power might have been tipped."

"Cool," Benji said.

Jules smiled. "Yes, Benjamin Hitchcock. Very cool.

There aren't many families who can say they went on vacation and saved the world, eh?"

A night later the family Hitchcock was on a plane headed home to Chicago. As opposed to their trip overseas, they flew direct. The long wait on the Philadelphia runway was ancient history, as were the greasy cheesesteaks, the connecting flights, and the arguments. Indeed, the Hitchcocks traveled back in style, first class, their reward from the French government for helping track down the MGF.

Best of all on this trip, when an exhausted Roger and Rebecca slept, it was with their hands entwined and their heads on each other's shoulders. Halfway across the Atlantic, Benji couldn't resist rubbing it in to his sister—just a little bit.

"Told ya," he said, nodding at his parents.

A row ahead, Rebecca sighed and pressed her head more closely against Roger's neck.

Maddy shot her brother a look. "First of all, no one likes a know-it-all. And second of all, it's not like the signs weren't all there to—"

"Come on," Benji interrupted. "Just admit you were wrong."

Maddy smiled. "I admit that you're a dork."

"Wow," Benji said. "Some things never change."

His sister turned back to her magazine. "Nope. Certain things never do."

Late that night the family pulled up to the house in their old minivan. Before swinging into the driveway, Roger idled on the street. Everything appeared to be as it always was: the grass, the trees, the mailbox, the driveway. But something felt different. Finally, Maddy broke the silence.

"Does anyone other than me think our house looks really strange?"

Roger nodded. "It does, doesn't it?"

"But it's still the same old house."

"It is," Benji said. "But we've changed. That's why it looks funny."

The family was silent. Benji had nailed it. Yes, the home itself was the same, but the people they had once been no longer existed.

"Well, Hitchcocks," Roger said. "Should we go inside and survey the damage?"

A moment later Roger pushed open the front door. The family held their collective breath, expecting the worst—instead the living room looked pretty much as they had left it.

"Not bad," Rebecca said.

"Yeah," Benji said. "Maybe we should do a house swap next summer."

"Not," Maddy said.

As the rest of the family headed toward their own rooms, Maddy walked down the hall to hers. At her door, she paused. Six days wasn't all that long. But it was plenty of time for a stranger to destroy her room—especially someone like the freak girl with tattoos who had stayed there. Had the so-called Chicago Veronique painted her walls black? Drawn a picture of a skull on the ceiling? Signed her name on the floor in blood? Anything seemed possible.

OK, Maddy thought. *Here goes.*

By the time she pushed open the door, Maddy was so certain that her room would be going to be trashed that it took her a moment to realize that it looked good. In fact, the girl with tattoos was even neater than she was. Maddy threw her suitcase on her bed, then couldn't resist quickly logging on to her computer. She had been out of internet touch for the past week, a veritable lifetime in the fast-moving life of a teenage girl. Indeed, she had more than three hundred emails. Even better was the subject line on one of the most recent: *Noah!!! Top Secret!!!* Maddy was about to click on it but then stopped. Before she jumped back into the world of Noah and the pool, there was something she wanted to do first.

True, her mother could still be annoying. But wasn't that the way with all mothers? Besides, her mother could be lots of other things, too. Good things. Over vacation, Maddy had seen her mom hang in there against all odds and drive like an action hero on a mountain road. She had even heard her admit how hard it was for her to watch Maddy grow up. Ironically, now that she was home, Maddy felt as though she wanted her mother more than ever: not necessarily to talk about boys—she had her friends for that—but to, well, just talk.

And so before Maddy checked her emails, she logged on to Facebook and typed in a search: *Rebecca Hitchcock*. She had never bothered to check her mother's profile before and was struck by the picture she had chosen, a casual shot from the previous year's vacation with her hair hanging loosely around her face. Best of all, she was smiling. Maddy smiled back, then moved her cursor to an icon she never would have imagined clicking a week earlier: *Add as Friend*.

Then came the scream—a piercing cry that shook the house. Maddy froze, heart pounding. Were the fake

Vadims still here? Terrified, Maddy rose to her feet—then she heard the scream again. This time she could identify its source. Benji. She ran down the hall and met her parents outside his room. Together, Roger, Rebecca, and Maddy barged in, fearing the worst. Instead, Benji was on his hands and knees, unharmed but in tears.

"What?" Maddy said. "What is it?"

"Look!" Benji said.

"At what?" Rebecca said. "The room is fine!"

"*Look!*" Benji shrieked.

Roger, Rebecca, and Maddy saw it at the same time. On his desk lay an enormous pile of Legos.

"My Lego Death Star!" Benji wailed. "It took me two full months to construct it!"

Roger, Rebecca, and Maddy exchanged a relieved sigh.

"Freak," Maddy said.

"You'll rebuild it, sport," Roger said. "Maybe make a Lego Universe out of it."

"Come on," Rebecca said. She rubbed Benji's back. "It was a long flight. Let's get something to eat."

A short while later the family was gathered around the kitchen table, feasting on thawed-in-the-oven frozen bagels with cream cheese—this time Roger had remembered to turn off the oven before they burned to a crisp.

"It was a great trip," Benji said. "But we didn't get to do half the things on my list."

Roger nodded. "You know what they say, Benj. If you wanna make God laugh, tell him your plans."

"I'm wondering," Maddy said. "Was that the best trip we've ever had?"

"Definitely," Rebecca said.

"Hold on," Roger said. "What about Bermuda? It wasn't as exciting, but the beach was beautiful."

"Yeah, the beach was nice," Maddy said. "But don't forget, I got the chicken pox."

"I got stung by an eel," Benji said.

Rebecca patted Roger's hand. "And you, my dear, lay in bed all week with a sunburn."

"Oh," Roger said. "I forgot about that."

"Anyway," Rebecca said with a yawn. "We can talk more tomorrow. I'm wiped. 'Night, everyone."

"'Night, hon. I'll be right up."

"Don't be long."

"'Night, Mom," Maddy said.

"'Night," Benji said. "Sleep well."

Rebecca walked to her room and, overcome by exhaustion, flopped down on the bed. A moment later something told her to get up. Like Maddy, she hadn't checked her email in a week. Though tempted to wait until morning, she eventually stumbled over to her computer, logged on, and checked her messages. The most recent one caught her eye immediately. Rebecca swallowed hard, then wiped away a tear. Then she clicked *Confirm*.

She'd happily be Maddy's friend on Facebook. She'd also try to be a better friend and a more understanding mother in day-to-day life.

Later that night Rebecca lay in Roger's arms, both moments from sleep.

"Let's never do another house swap," Roger murmured.

"You twisted my arm."

A moment passed. The room was perfectly still.

"I hope the police are easy on the Vadims," Rebecca said. "They weren't bad people; they just made some bad decisions."

"I think they're cooperating with the authorities," Roger said. "They'll probably get off with a hand slap."

"I hope," Rebecca said. "Their kids were cute."

Another moment passed. Roger began to doze, his head buried in his wife's hair.

"You know where I want to go next, Mr. Hitchcock? Rio."

"De Janeiro? What's there?"

"The Olympics, for one. Two thousand sixteen."

"Wow, you should start training now."

"No," Rebecca said. "It'll be a giant family adventure."

"I'm in," Roger said. "How many frequent-flier miles do we have left?"

Rebecca didn't answer. She had finally dozed off. Roger gave her a soft kiss on the forehead, then closed his own eyes.

Rio, he thought. Had possibilities.